Lynn KB Anderson is a retired clerical assistant for the NHS. Prior to that, Lynn had various positions including a care assistant at a care home in Waterloo. Lynn enjoys watching quiz shows and has appeared on three in the past. Lynn is from Liverpool and is now living in Southport with her husband, John, who is also retired. She has two sons from a previous marriage and five grandchildren. *The Good Life* is Lynn's first novel; she has always wanted to write but never got the opportunity till she saw an advert for a writing course in her local book shop. Since joining the course in January 2018, Lynn has written three novels. She hopes *The Good Life* will be successful, after which she hopes to publish the other two. She is, at this moment, writing the first book of a three-book saga.

Lynn KB Anderson

# THE GOOD LIFE

AUSTIN MACAULEY PUBLISHERS™

LONDON * CAMBRIDGE * NEW YORK * SHARJAH

A CIP catalogue record for this title is available from the British Library.

ISBN 9781528995436 (Paperback)
ISBN 9781528995443 (ePub e-book)

www.austinmacauley.com

First Published 2022
Austin Macauley Publishers Ltd®
1 Canada Square
Canary Wharf
London
E14 5AA

I would like to thank Sally-Anne Tapier-Bowes, my tutor on the Plath Novel Writing Course 9, who has taught me a great deal over the two years I have attended. I would also like to thank my husband, John, who has been very patient and has been my sounding board for my many characters. He has been patient and very encouraging towards my ambition to become an author.

# Chapter 1

I first met her on the beach; the sun was just disappearing over the horizon turning the world aflame with golden light as she sauntered along the silvery sand. She was stunning with her long black hair flowing in the soft breeze over her slim shoulders. As she drew near me, I stopped to gaze upon this goddess. She wore a flowing dress of bright colours which showed off her golden limbs. She stopped and saw me watching her. Her crescent-shaped eyebrows inclined slightly.

"Do you want to ask me a question? Are you lost?" she asked in her delicious soft accent.

I was 14 going on 15. Not quite a man yet, but I had the yearnings of a man, I was tongue tied I could not stop staring at her. After a long silence I smiled.

"No, I'm not lost just taking time to myself. My name is Jimmy."

The goddess smiled showing her luminous white teeth. I noticed her small, scrolled ears and her pert nose.

"Would you like to walk with me?"

I didn't hesitate. I took her small delicate hand into my large hand, and we strolled on. Her name was Celeste; she was 22 and from Milan. I lied and told her I was eighteen. I looked eighteen. I was nearly six foot and my voice had broken. The moon had hidden behind a lonely cloud hiding its light. I felt her shiver, so I removed my shirt and placed it around her slim shoulders. I could smell her feminine perfume, which sent my senses reeling. I felt an ache in my groin. I took my courage in both hands and kissed her fully on her lips. The beach was quiet except for the swishing of the tide ebbing to-and-fro to the shore. She kissed me, and her lips tasted like saccharine, they were soft and luscious it was my first adult kiss. We lay down in the sand where she taught me how to please a woman. Later, as she lay in my arms, I was smiling pleased with myself I was now a man. I never saw Celeste again, but I would never forget that first time for the rest of my life.

## Liverpool, April 1957

"Christine, I'm not telling you again get a move on you'll be late for school."

Madge Bennett pushed a strand of her brown but greying hair behind her ear. Her daughter Christine, Chrissy to her friends, was always dawdling while getting ready for school. Unlike her brother Norman, also known as Norm, who was no trouble; he was in his last year at school and was hoping to pass his leaving exams so he could attend the technical college in Old Swan. He wanted to follow his dad, also named Norman, as a fitter in the Automatic in Edge Lane.

"Mam, can I have more toast?" Gerry, her youngest, pleaded who had the appetite of a horse.

"No Gerry, the rest are for your sister when she finally gets down the stairs."

"Sorry Mam," Chrissy said slightly out of breath after running down the stairs. "I had a mark on my blouse and had to get it out."

"Well, hurry up! Your tea is cold and there's no time to make more. You will have to buck up when you start work my girl."

Chrissy wasn't that fussy on school, but she enjoyed English and domestic science and seeing her friends. Her best friend, May Makin, lived next door in Northumberland Terrace Everton. They had been friends since toddlers and were more like sisters. Another thing Chrissy did not like about school was that she was the smallest girl in her year and the boys teased her and called her 'Titch', which she hated. Chrissy hoped she wasn't going to take after her mam for being small, she loved her mum who was still pretty but very petite. Chrissy liked that instead of 'Titch'. She overheard her dad call her mum his petite girl.

"Chrissy, Chrissy!" May ran up to her. "I have been calling you for ages. Didn't you hear me?"

May was only two months younger than Chrissy but was taller and slimmer unlike Chrissy, who was more rounded which her dad called 'puppy fat'.

The school bell rang for a break. The weather was cool but sunny, so they would be allowed outside for 15 minutes. No sooner had Chrissy and May stepped out they were met by the boys from the third year.

"Here comes Titch and Skinny Malink." Which was May's nickname.

"Just ignore them, Chrissy," told her friend. "They are just stupid boys."

"Hope you don't think I'm stupid," a voice behind her said with laughter.

Chrissy turned and looked into chocolate brown eyes with a glint of amber. This boy was different from the other boys; he was lanky, muscular and seemed more like a man than a boy. She hadn't noticed him before, how she could forget that wide smile which showed perfect white teeth and those eyes that were now looking deep into her soul as if he was searching for some unknown secret she kept there.

"I asked, what is your name?"

Chrissy came out of her trance to tell him her name.

"My name is Jimmy." He turned to the other boys who looked at him with hero worship. "Leave her alone. From now on, there will be no name calling. Otherwise you will have me to answer to." At that moment, the bell rang. Again, Jimmy smiled and said, "See ya again, Chrissy."

May asked Chrissy, "Now where did he spring from? He is so handsome. Wonder what year he is in?"

After school, as Chrissy and May walked home, they saw Jimmy on the other side of the road with some other boys presumably from his class. May recognised some and thought they might be in their last year at school.

"Our brothers might know Jimmy. Why don't we ask them if they know him and find out more about him?"

"I don't know," Chrissy replied. "Our Norman is funny about stuff like that. He might want to know why I'm asking about him. Anyway, what's the point? If he is in his last year, he won't want to be bothered about us we are only 12. He must be the same age as our brothers who are nearly 15."

May thought to herself, *Well, I'm asking. Because 15 or not, I want to find out more about Jimmy.*

Little did May know that her friend was thinking the same thoughts.


**May 1957**

Chrissy hadn't set eyes on Jimmy since that time in the playground, she had found out from her friend May that his name was Jimmy Cartwright and he was 14, but 15 in July. He lived in Breck Road Anfield, and his dad was a docker. May had quizzed her brother Arthur, which did arouse his suspicions, but she explained she was asking for Chrissy. Arthur, who had just turned 15 had his hopes on passing his exams and was looking to join the police cadets. He was the right height and had a big frame, which according to his mam, looked like his late dad. With his dark blue eyes and blond hair, he stood out. He liked

Chrissy but now she was just like a little sister and that was as far as it went, he knew Jimmy Cartwright who was in the same year as him they were both in the A-stream class. Jimmy was clever and could do most sports, especially football. He played for the school team but sometimes he would cry off saying he had something to do at home. The girls loved him which made some of the other boys jealous, but he still had many friends because he didn't boast about his skill, he also helped others if they struggled with a certain subject. He also seemed to have a lot of cash but was generous. In fact, Arthur thought he didn't seem to have any faults at all.

It was during lunch time when Chrissy met Jimmy again. She was sitting in the corner of the playground reading her book by herself because May was off sick. Chrissy heard footsteps and looked up and saw those dark brown eyes with a hint of amber that she had not forgotten.

"Hi, Chrissy."

She paused, not knowing what to say after a while she managed a 'Hi'. He asked if he could sit beside her and she moved up, her senses reeled his knee had slightly touched hers and he had some kind of aftershave on, which smelt lovely.

"Where is your friend May?"

Chrissy felt disappointed because he had asked about her friend.

"Oh, she is not well. I'm not sure if she will be back before the Whit holidays."

"Are you going anywhere? If the weather is fine, me and my mates are going for a bike ride over the water. Do you and your friend have bikes? You could come with us we will make sure you are safely returned home."

Chrissy felt excited at being asked out by Jimmy even though they would be with his mates. She then remembered they were going away to her aunty Helen in Southport her excitement turned to sorrow.

"Sorry, I can't. We are going away."

"Oh well, never mind. Maybe some other time, hey."

He then got up and walked away that would be the last time for many years she would see and speak to her first love again because in that moment she realised she would never love anyone else.

# Chapter 2

## Liverpool February 1963

"Maud, where is our Chrissy? It's half ten, I thought she was helping you with getting the parlour ready for her birthday," Norman Bennett Sr asked his wife. He had just finished his breakfast of bacon, sausages, egg and fried bread and was reading the last evenings Liverpool Echo. Norman enjoyed his weekends off. It was Saturday. He had a good lie in till 9:30 because he thought that was late enough to be lying in bed. Norman was still in his prime for his age at 45. He was fit; a muscular six feet tall and still had a full head of dark brown hair, which was greying at the temples. He was a strict father, especially with his daughter Chrissy, but he was also kind and generous. He loved his family and was proud of his eldest son, also called Norman, who was an apprentice at the Automatic. His thoughts were interrupted by his youngest son Gerry running into the kitchen.

"Dad, dad! Georgie has just told me his dad is taking him to the game at Goodison, can we go?"

"How does he know son? His dad hasn't mentioned anything to me," he replied with a smile. Norman knew they were going as well but he was keeping it as a surprise.

"Georgie heard his dad talking to his mum."

"He shouldn't be listening in to adults talking. We will see."

Chrissy had finished helping her mum and decided to go next door to see her best friend May. Chrissy was looking forward to her 18th birthday party at her house but was more excited about the visit to the Grafton in West Derby Road. The popular dance hall was a favourite of people of most ages and this was going to be Chrissy's first visit. She loved all the popular music especially the Beatles. She didn't own a record player so could not buy any records. She was saving up from her wages she earned working in a factory in Edge Lane. After giving her keep, Chrissy was left with 15 shillings, which she spent on clothes and make-up and saving the rest in a post office account. Chrissy, who had been small while at school, had now grown taller and had lost her puppy fat. She was now a slim, attractive, young woman with shoulder length dark wavy hair brown eyes and full lips which were always smiling. Her friend May had an older brother, Arthur, and he had asked her out on many occasions. Chrissy liked Arthur but was not really interested in him as a boyfriend. Chrissy had asked Arthur to go with them to the Grafton because her friends from work were going some with their boyfriends and hoped Arthur might take an interest in one of them. Her brother, Norm, told her he was bringing a girlfriend with him which surprised Chrissy because he hadn't mentioned having a girlfriend before.

### Grafton 16<sup>th</sup> February

Chrissy was having a great time the live band were great and were playing all the popular songs from the Beatles, Searchers, Gerry and the Pacemakers, and many more. She had enjoyed the party at her house but had to make do with the radio, it was good of her parents to let her have a party, but this was more exciting with the live music and more of her friends. She had had loads of dances some even with Arthur and had her first drink which was a Babycham, which was quite nice. She wore a dark blue shift dress with a wide white collar matched with a white cardigan and blue strap shoes with a small heel and finished off her outfit with a white beaded necklace. Chrissy was having a rest and was watching her friends enjoying themselves when she heard someone behind her asking. "Titch, is that you?"

Chrissy turned around and looked up into a pair of chocolate brown eyes with a glint of amber, eyes that she remembered from six years ago.

"Jimmy?"

He had grown a lot taller which made her strain her neck to look at him. He dwarfed the other boys who were here tonight; he was broader in his shoulders; he was wearing a tailored blue suit with no collar a dark blue shirt and a thin white tie he looked so smart. Her heart was performing somersaults and she felt her pulse quickening.

"I'm not Titch anymore. I've grown now," Chrissy felt childish saying that, but she couldn't think what else to say.

"You certainly have. I'm sorry I called you Titch. It was the first thing that came into my head, I was *that* surprised to see you. It's Chrissy, isn't it?"

12

She couldn't believe he had remembered her name after all those years.

"Yes, it's Chrissy. Where did you disappear to? You were asking me to go on a bike ride then you were gone no one knew where."

"My dad got a job as a stevedore on the docks in London. It was too good an opportunity to miss bit of a mad rush really had no time to tell anyone."

Jimmy noticed the badge pinned to her cardigan.

"I see you're celebrating a birthday, how old are you? If I'm not being rude asking your age."

Chrissy looked down and flushed.

"That was May, she pinned it on. I turned 18 yesterday we had a small party at my house, then decided to come here tonight."

"I'm glad you did. Come on, let's have a dance."

Chrissy followed him onto the dancefloor her heart was still doing somersaults. After a couple of dances to the songs of *Love me do* and *the young ones,* they returned to the bar and found her brother and his girlfriend, Jean, her friend May and Arthur.

Chrissy introduced Jimmy and asked if they remembered him from school.

"Yes," Arthur replied with a scowl. "When did you get back to Liverpool, Cartwright?"

"Three months ago. My mam missed her family and friends and was feeling depressed she didn't like London, so Dad took a lower rank to get back onto Liverpool docks. Hi Norman. Hi Jean. Long-time no see, what yer all doing now?"

Arthur gave him a hard stare. "I'm on the police force now. Still training, but I will be finished soon."

Chrissy looked at Arthur. Why was he being so unfriendly to Jimmy? After discussing their various jobs Jimmy asked Chrissy for another dance it was a slow one to Cliff Richards, *The next time.* Jimmy took her hand and led her to the dancefloor. She looked back and saw Arthur scowling and shaking his head. *I can dance with anyone,* she thought. *I'm not your girlfriend.*

As they danced, the lights had been dimmed and the rotating-coloured globe hanging from the high ceiling gave the dance hall a cosy romantic aura. She could smell his aftershave which somehow sent her senses reeling with a passion she had never felt before. With his collar-length hair slicked down with Brylcreem, he looked like a film star. She could feel his warm breath on her cheek and as he held her close, she could feel his hard lean body hot against her own. She wanted this dance to last forever but sadly it ended. Instead of releasing her, he kept her enfolded in his arms and whispered.

"Chrissy, I must go now. Can you meet me next Saturday outside of Blair Hall on Walton Road at 7:30?"

"Yes," she replied without any hesitation. She felt elated he wanted to see her again he was the most handsome and well-dressed man here tonight. Her heart was now beating much harder she felt it might burst from her body.

"What was he saying?" Arthur asked when she returned from the dancefloor. Jimmy had left the dance hall with two men.

"Nothing to do with you, Arthur Makin. Why were you so nasty to him?"

"There is something about him I don't trust. How can he afford clothes like that? He is only an insurance salesman and who were those men he left with just now? Just you be careful Chrissy, you don't really know him, do you?"

"You knew him at school, and you liked him then," May replied.

"I don't know. He seems a decent bloke, it's just your suspicious coppers mind," Norm said.

Chrissy kept silent. She didn't want Arthur and her brother to know she was meeting him, but she would confide in May later.

# Chapter 3

As Jimmy left the Grafton, his thoughts turned to the task he was about to take on. He wasn't very happy when he saw Nosey Jones and Roachy enter the Grafton, it meant he was wanted by his boss, Gaffer Goff, who was a notorious money lender who went to extreme measures to get his debtors to pay even if they couldn't. His rates were that high that many found it difficult to repay him so he would get his sidekicks to beat them up and take their belongings. Jimmy's role was to try and persuade them to pay before it resorted to violence most times it would work and he was happy. When it turned violent, Jimmy just walked away and let them get on with it. He had a job selling insurance, but the money wasn't enough to give him the good things in life which was why he worked for Goff. On this occasion, they were to visit a woman who owed ten pounds.

"I don't know why the gaffer has sent you two along I can deal with her myself I'm not letting you lay a finger on a woman for god's sake."

"You're too soft. The gaffer wants his money it's doubled now because she has taken too long to pay. You have given her two chances and she hasn't paid. Now he wants us to go to make sure she does pay," Nosey Jones told Jimmy.

Jimmy didn't like working for Goff, but the money he earned was very good. He could afford the best clothes, the best restaurants and clubs in Liverpool he also owned a car. He didn't usually visit the Grafton, but he was glad he went tonight. He remembered Chrissy when she was a small dumpy looking kid, but even then, she had something about her. What a change in her tonight she wasn't what you call beautiful but she was a looker she had grown taller and slimmer she had warm brown eyes lovely dark shiny hair with a warm genuine smile on her full luscious lips and she felt good in his arms. Chrissy wasn't normally his type. He liked his women to be sexy and easy to lay, but Chrissy was different, if he ever wanted to settle down. Well, not for a while. He was still only twenty, she would be the type he would marry.

As Jimmy climbed out of his red *lotus* elan, he turned to look at his pride and joy it was two years old and he had bought it in London from one of his dad's cronies for a really good price. He wasn't sure where it had come from, but it didn't let it bother him. He was just putting the hood up it was a wet night with a penetrating chill, when he heard a young voice shout.

"Mister, mister can I look after yer car for only six pence."

Jimmy smiled at the young lad who looked to be about nine or ten. He had no coat just a jumper with holes, short pants and boots that were too big for him. He looked as if he hadn't seen soap and water for weeks. Jimmy had come to the run-down area of Great Homer Street where there was a big slum clearance. There were gaping holes between each house where the ravages of war had left their mark. Jimmy despaired of his home city. He asked the lad if he could take care of his car by himself.

"You look a bit small lad."

"I'm alright, mister. I can take care of me self."

"OK" Jimmy laughed. "If it's alright, when I return, I will pay you."

Jimmy told Nosey and Roachy to remain in their own car till he wanted them. He then knocked on the door of a rundown small, terraced house, but unlike the others, the curtains were clean the step was well scrubbed, and the windows were clean. He knocked again.

After a while, the door slowly opened to a small gap where a small voice with an Irish accent asked, "Yea, why are yer knocking at this time of night what do yer want?"

"Sorry Mrs O'Reilly, it's Jimmy. Can I come in and have a talk?"

Jimmy knew Mary O'Reilly. It was him who had managed to arrange the loan for her. She had three kids and was expecting again. Her husband, Paddy, was in and out of work and most of that time he spent what little they had on drink. Mary took in washing to make more money and in desperation, had approached Jimmy for a loan as she knew he worked for Gaffer Goff. The sum she loaned was for five pounds but had rapidly raised to ten pounds because of the high interest he charged.

"Oh, come in, Jimmy," Mary opened the door wider to let him in.

Jimmy noticed how clean the house was kept. She was a proud woman. Mary was small in stature and very wiry she had a care worn look, but Jimmy could tell she must have once been pretty.

"Sorry Jimmy, I only have five pounds. Paddy found the money and disappeared with it. I haven't seen him for a couple of days."

He looked around and thought if those two thugs got involved, they would take everything she owned even the beds.

"Look, Mary. Goff wants his money. Now his thugs are outside, and you will have sod all left. I will pay the 10 pounds; you can pay me back whatever you can. I won't charge as much interest but please don't say a word otherwise that's the end of me, I'm doing this for a favour because Paddy is a bastard I will ask my mates to look out for him and send him home."

"Oh, Jimmy thank you. I will pay you as soon as I can. You're a good lad, Jimmy."

He returned to his car Nosey and Roachy were standing next to their car.

"Well, did she pay you then? If not, we will get the van and clear the house and give that Irish good for nothing Paddy a good hiding," Nosey shouted.

"No need for that." He waved the two five-pound notes in their faces. "Paddy won on the horses and Mary nicked the money from his coat pocket while he slept, so you can leave them alone."

They looked disappointed that there wasn't going to be a good fight and got back into their cars and drove away. He looked around for the young lad then all of a sudden, he ran from the back entry.

"Here I am mister. I was looking after yer car and those two men chased me but honest, I looked after it."

Jimmy smiled and held out half a crown, the lad's eyes opened wide and asked.

"Is that for me?"

"Yea of course, lad. You did well, my car is fine."

The lad put out his grubby hand and took the money as he ran off down the road he shouted, "Ta mister."

Jimmy climbed into his car and drove off thinking of his date next Saturday with Chrissy.

Chrissy and her companions were leaving the Grafton it was now 11:30, she was tired but happy she had enjoyed herself tonight with her friends and her brother, who was now escorting herself and May home. Arthur had gone off with a girl he had been dancing with most of the night, they were walking behind Norm who had his arm around Jean's waist. May was taller than Chrissy, who had blond hair cropped into the style of Cilla Black the lass from Scottie Road.

May had wanted to dye her hair the same colour as Cilla but her mum had said no. She was lucky she was letting her have it cut short. May had attended night school to learn how to type and learn shorthand and now she worked in Littlewooods Pools in Edge Lane.

"I think our Arthur has gone off in a huff, he wasn't happy about Jimmy turning up out of the blue he still wants to take you out."

"I'm sorry, May. I do like your Arthur but only as a friend. I don't want you to tell anyone yet, Jimmy asked me to meet him next week outside of Blair Hall and I'm going."

"What are you going to tell your mum and dad when you get all dolled up?"

"I don't know yet. I might say I'm going to meet another friend from work I don't want to involve you in any lies. I just know Dad will want to meet Jimmy before he will let me go out with him. Doesn't he know its 1963 and not 1863? He is so old fashioned, it's not fair. I have to be home by midnight while our Norm can arrive home any time. Mum says it's because he is a man, but I don't see what difference that should make."

After her little rant, Chrissy laughed and said, "I can't wait till next Saturday to see Jimmy."

May was not sure about the fact her friend was meeting Jimmy behind her parents back. They hadn't seen Jimmy for years and didn't know him that well, he was handsome and seemed to have money by the way he was dressed, but he was an insurance salesman and May didn't think he would earn that much to afford tailored suits, her brother and Norm bought their suits off the peg. She wasn't jealous of her friend, she just wanted to look out for her best friend. May kept these thoughts to herself because she didn't want to spoil the obvious joy Chrissy was feeling.

# Chapter 4

## Monday 18<sup>th</sup> February The Grove Inn

Jimmy entered the Grove Inn, which was located near the Dock Road. The pub was run down with an obvious sign of neglect; paint peeling from the door, two windows boarded up. He was amazed it was still open for business. It had just turned 5:30, so the bar only housed the usual scallies; the daily boozers who had little else to do with their time. The ale was cheap if a little watery and the spirits had unrecognisable labels. The inside was no better threadbare carpet which was so sticky with spilt ale that your feet stuck to it, dark wallpaper that was peeling from the wall and low lights so the drinkers could not notice how bad and dirty it was, but then again, they wouldn't care. This was the place where Gaffer Goff held his money lending business in the room at the back, he knew Goff didn't live around here so he couldn't understand why he chose this god forsaken place. He walked into the back room, which was also badly lit, it was in the same bad condition as the bar but had no carpet. In the middle of the room was a desk with a swivel chair behind it and in the front of the desk stood a red plastic chair. In the corner stood a portable electric fire with two bars which gave off little heat. At the both ends of the desk stood two hulks who were Goff's minders, one had cropped hair to his scalp, a broken nose and cauliflower ears. Jimmy knew he was an ex-boxer who was so punch drunk he had to be told everything twice, but he looked scary. The other minder was the opposite, he had long blond hair which was tied back his features were perfect, he had cool blue eyes which stared hard at you and had an evil glint. Sitting in the swivel chair was Goff, he was in his 50s, had little hair, which he combed over his bald head, he overindulged which left him with a large stomach which he struggled to keep from bursting through his waist coat. He had a double chin and small piggy eyes and a wet loose mouth. He was well dressed in a large sheepskin coat dark pinstriped suit and brown leather shoes. He was smoking a fat cigar and had a bottle of best whisky on the desk. Jimmy couldn't stand looking at his fat smug face.

"Ahh Jimmy, I hear that Irish tart has paid her debt in full which I find hard to believe, did she go on the streets? Ha Ha must have taken her weeks to get that amount. Come on lad, how did she manage it?"

Jimmy saw his minders smirk.

"Paddy won on the horses, and she nicked it while he slept."

"Funny. I heard he had gone missing I didn't know he had won on the horses. I usually get to hear stuff like that it gets round. You know everyone knows the Irish bastard, you know him don't you lads?" he turned to his minders who had started to laugh along with their boss.

Jimmy stayed silent he didn't like Paddy either but felt sorry for his poor suffering wife and kids. He pulled out two fivers from his pocket.

"Here is the money. I'll take my share." He placed the two fivers on the table and Goff took out his wallet, placed the money in and gave Jimmy three pound notes. "What next?" he asked, wanting to get this meeting over and done with he felt uneasy under the watchful stare of one of his minders.

"OK then, let's get down to business." Goff had now lost his humour and had a serious look upon his face which worried Jimmy.

"I want you to take Nosey and Roachy with you to the Bully. I want you to go to Lenny Thompsons flat and either persuade him to pay up or face Nosey and Roachy. Wait, hang on. I'll send these two along with you instead, you'll have a better chance to get the money. He owes me a fifty. It's got serious now. I'm not waiting any longer I've got a feeling he is going to do a runner."

The 'Bully' was the bull ring off London Road; it was a block of flats built into a circle with a bit of grass in the centre. It had two entrances and was notorious for the hard cases who lived there it was hard to enter unless you were known or knew someone who lived there. Jimmy didn't like the idea that Goff was willing to give up his minders to get his money, he took his minders everywhere, he had recruited them a while back after one of his debtor's family tried to kill him when he left the Grove. Luckily for him, a copper on the beat saw the struggle and managed to grab the attacker's knife and arrest him.

"OK Gaffer, when do you want me to go, tonight?"

"No. Go now before he knows what is happening. I'll stay here till you have finished then send the lads back here you don't have to return here just make sure you get something. Go in the van in case there is anything worth taking. Wait outside while I have a word with the lads."

After Jimmy left the room, Goff turned to his minders and told them to teach Thompson a lesson whether he pays or not. The minders smiled and rubbed their hands in glee, it was a while since they had had a good fight and were looking forward to one soon.

They arrived at the bullring and parked the van inside the courtyard. There was a gang of teenagers hanging around smoking. They stopped talking and stared at the van and Jimmy then ignored him when they saw the two minders climbing out the van. They were not chancing going head-to-head with those two bruisers. Jimmy and the minders walked up the three flights of stone stairs in the gloomy concrete building, which were dimly lit and smelled of dried vomit and pee. They stepped out onto the balcony of the second floor and made their way to Lenny's flat. Jimmy used the knocker and gave two loud knocks, after a while when there was no answer. The two minders pushed Jimmy aside and kicked the door in.

They entered a small hallway with a load of cardboard boxes covering the floor, on a hanger hung a grey mac and a brown cap, they went into the living room which housed an electric fire a black plastic settee and a table covered in dirty dishes and an ashtray full of used cigarette ends, one of the minders muttered, "Dirty bastard," as they looked around the unkept room, they searched the kitchen that had a built-in-cupboard that was bare an electric cooker which was covered in grease, what the hell has he been spending his money on thought Jimmy how could anyone live in this filth he couldn't fathom.

The two minders went into the bedroom where they found a metal single bed with a thin stained mattress a dirty sheet and a thin brown army blanket crumpled up at the bottom, in the corner stood a wardrobe with no doors there were no clothes inside then they noticed a handle sticking out from under the bed, the ugly minder pointed to a built in cupboard and put his finger to his lips they crept over to the cupboard and pulled open the door, crouching inside was Lenny who was wearing an expensive looking suit and black leather shoes, they shouted for Jimmy to join them then dragged Lenny out by his legs and pushed him up against the wall.

"Sorry, sorry don't hurt me. I have Goff's money I was going to pay him tomorrow honest."

Jimmy walked in and shook his head. "Why were you hiding Lenny?"

"I thought you were the cops."

The minders punched him and hissed, "Liar." Lenny cried out in pain.

Jimmy walked to the bed leaned down pulled out a small suitcase opened it up and found new shirts, jumpers, trousers and underneath a wad of five and ten-pound notes tied up with an elastic band.

"Whose money is this?" asked Jimmy. "There must be hundreds here."

"Some of it is to pay Goff. The rest is mine."

"Where did you get this amount from?" asked Jimmy as he proceeded to count the notes.

"I robbed it from a betting shop."

"There is two hundred here, were you doing a runner?"

"No, no I told yer. I was going to pay Goff."

Jimmy took a fifty from the wad. "Right then, I'm off." Then walked out the flat. As he left, he could hear the screams of Lenny. No one bothered to come out to see what the shouting was they had learned to mind their own business living here.

Minutes later, the two minders returned to the van removing the thick metal knuckle dusters which had traces of blood. Laughing, they waved the wad of notes in Jimmy's face.

"Look Cartwright, you have the Gaffer's money, we're keeping the rest so keep your mouth shut. What the Gaffer don't know won't hurt him."

"I don't care what you do, he won't hear nothing from me. Now give us a lift home and tell Goff I will see him tomorrow."

When Jimmy was dropped home and the van drove off, he smiled. So the minders were not true to the Gaffer, which served him right. What had happened to Lenny? He didn't really care it had been a long night and he wanted his bed.

Chrissy was sitting in the kitchen. The Bennett family had just finished their tea. Her mum and dad were sitting in the red moquette fireside chairs drinking tea; Norman and Gerry sitting at the table, Gerry reading the Beano and Norm reading the Liverpool Echo on the sports page.

"I'm taking your mum to the pictures on Saturday night after the match. Chrissy, will you look after our Gerry?"

"Uh." Chrissy's face fell. "I was thinking of going out this Saturday, Dad. With a friend from work." She didn't want to miss her date with Jimmy.

"Now come on Chrissy, how often do me and your mum get a chance to go out? It's only one Saturday."

Chrissy was just about to reluctantly give in when Norman surprisingly came to her rescue.

"I'll stay with Gerry, if it's OK for me to bring a friend."

"Which friend is that, son?" his mother asked.

"It's my girlfriend, Mum. Her name is Jean, who used to be in my class at school, we met each other a couple of months ago."

There was a moments silence till his dad asked. "Why keep her a secret so long?"

"We didn't think our relationship was serious enough to tell our parents and Jean was not confident enough to meet you all, but that changed now. I want you to meet her before you go out on Saturday."

"OK son," replied his mum. "Are you sure she won't mind staying in to mind Gerry? Maybe she can come for tea then we can get to know the young lass properly, this is the first girl you have bought home."

Norman told them she lived in Bootle with her mum and younger sister and she worked in woollies in town on the make-up counter. "Jean is gorgeous and has a lovely and lively personality and she livens up my life."

"We look forward to meeting her," his parents said while smiling.

Chrissy was stunned, she had met Jean once at the Grafton Chrissy's first impression of her was Jean was good for a laugh, but she didn't seem the right kind of girl for her quiet serious brother.

# Chapter 5

### Blair Hall

Chrissy was so excited that she had splashed out on some new make-up and bought a new winter coat in ruby red. She had received money from her parents and brother for her birthday, which she was intending to use for a record player, but she had wanted to look her best for Jimmy so had decided to buy a coat instead. She was early; she didn't want to chance missing the bus, so decided to catch the earlier one she now had to wait another ten minutes. Blair Hall was a dance hall on the second floor of the Co-Op on Walton Road; the basement housed furniture and a chemist, on the ground floor, they sold groceries and soft furnishings and the first floor housed the Co-Op offices and the bank. The entrance to the dance hall was in Christopher Street, which was where Chrissy was now waiting. She glanced at her watch and noticed it was thirty-five minutes past seven and began to feel nervous. *What if he hadn't been serious or maybe he had changed his mind.* As she was looking down the street, she noticed a small red car pull up in front of her it was one of those that had a hood you could pull up and take down. She didn't take much notice of the driver because she was busy looking down the street. The driver climbed out and walked up behind her as she was now looking up Walton Road.

"Chrissy."

She jumped. "Oh Jimmy, where did you come from? I didn't see you coming."

Jimmy laughed. "Sorry I frightened you. I was right in front of you in the car."

"That was you in the car who does it belong to?"

"It's mine."

"You have your own car?"

"Yes," Jimmy smiled. "Come on, it's starting to rain, let's get inside."

The hall wasn't very busy when they entered. Jimmy took her coat and led her to a table.

"What do you drink?"

"Can I have a babycham."

"I will get you something better than that."

"No thank you, that will do."

When he returned with the drinks, the hall had started to fill up and she was glad they had arrived early to get a good table. Chrissy was so enthralled with the idea she was with Jimmy that she didn't know what to say. Jimmy broke the silence.

"Well, tell what you have been doing with your life since leaving school."

After telling him where she worked and about her family, he told her about his jobs in London, working for a cobbler, then in the dock's office as a clerk. When he spoke of his mum, she could tell he was very fond of her, he told her his dad was a typical docker, rough and ready liked to have a drink but was good to his wife and son.

"I'm surprised you haven't already got a boyfriend, a good-looking lass like you."

"I have had boyfriends but not serious. My dad is quite strict and told me I'm too young to have a serious relationship. Arthur keeps asking me out, but I'm not interested in him in that way."

"I don't blame you. Don't know why he was so aggressive to me last week."

"Arthur is just jealous that I danced with you. He's OK really. You must have a good job to be able to own a car."

Jimmy told her about his job as an insurance salesman but declined to tell her of his side-line working for Goff, he had just met her and she might be put off.

"I get a bonus when I sell more insurance."

Chrissy looked at his clothes he was wearing; a white polo necked jumper, blue drainpipe jeans and brown winkle picker shoes. Chrissy thought he must be a good salesman to afford to have his own car and he was still only 20.

After dancing and chatting freely, Chrissy was enjoying herself. The atmosphere had been good but was now turning nasty, a group of young lads had arrived and were bothering the girlfriends of a group of friends, one of the friends told the interlopers to leave his girl alone and had a bottle thrown at him drenching him in beer, his mates had retaliated and the group had picked up

25

chairs and threw them, there was mayhem the men on the door had run in and started throwing punches, girls started screaming, Jimmy grabbed Chrissy's hand.

"Let's get out of here while we can." He ran to get their coats, and both ran down the stairs into the street.

The rain was heavy and a spray was blown into their faces by the wind. Chrissy now upset and crying was struggling to put on her coat. Jimmy opened the car door and bundled her in, his hair was dripping wet and his jacket clinging to his body. Chrissy shivered. He turned the engine on and turned up the heater.

He turned to her. "I'm sorry I shouldn't have taken you there."

"It's not your fault, it was those hooligans who spoilt it. I was enjoying myself."

They both stared at each other their hair now a mess clinging to their scalp, rain dripping off the end of their noses, they both burst out laughing. "Are you any warmer now, Chrissy?"

"Yes, thanks Jimmy."

"I had better get you home to get dry."

They were almost by Chrissy's when Jimmy asked if he could park somewhere because he had a present to give her for her birthday. They parked in a street which was dimly lit he turned off the engine then turned and reached behind his seat then pulled out a bag which he placed on her lap, she reached inside and pulled out two record albums, one was by a singer by the name of Tony Bennett and another by Etta James, she looked at Jimmy.

"I haven't heard of these singers what do they sing?"

"Tony Bennett is an American singer who sings pop standards big band and jazz a bit like Frank Sinatra this album has some good songs on, *the good life* is one of my favourites. Etta James is a black American female who sings blues and soul. Listen to *at last,* I think you would like that one, as you can see this this is my kind of music I have them at home I'm not too fussed on rock and roll and pop they are OK I like the Beatles but I prefer to listen to these and more. I hope you don't think I'm pushing my music tastes onto you just listen and make your own mind up."

"Thanks Jimmy I would love to, but I haven't a record player I've been saving but I needed to buy a new coat the one I have now I wanted to look smart, are they yours? I don't want to take them off you if I can't play them."

"It's OK. I have more at home. I got these from a mate who is a cabin steward on the SS Sylvania, it sails to New York and he buys them from record stores and sells them over here keep them till you can buy a record player."

"Thanks Jimmy, I will I look forward to hearing them." Chrissy told him about Norm bringing Jean around for tea. "Mum and Dad were surprised when they first saw Jean. She is so outgoing and loud she wore loads of make-up and wore a tight blouse and skirt, after a while they got used to her and our Gerry was smitten because she had bought him comics and chocolate, but I can't understand why she would be interested in our Norm, he is so quiet and serious."

Jimmy thought the same he remembered her from their schooldays, and she had a reputation with the boys he kept quiet it wasn't his problem. Norm would find out soon enough the kind of girl she was.

"Oh well, they say opposites attract. They may be good for each other; she will bring him out of his shell."

He took the bag from Chrissy and took her in his arms his warm lips gently touching hers, it was a gentle kiss at first and Chrissy was enjoying the new sensations her body was feeling. This was her first proper kiss and it was Jimmy's lips which were giving her these feelings, she responded by putting her arms around his neck and kissed him, his kisses then became more passionate and demanding she pushed him away not because she didn't like his kisses, she was scared of what might happen if she didn't stop now.

His breath was rasping as he muttered, "Sorry Chrissy, I didn't mean to frighten you."

"You didn't...well a bit. I did enjoy your kisses, but you were getting a bit rough. I'm not that kind of girl."

"Let's get you home. Can we meet next Friday? I will take you for something to eat then a club. Shall I pick you up from yours?"

"No, not yet. My dad will sit you down and question you. I think we should wait till we have been going steady first that's if you want to see me again."

He looked downcast. "Are you ashamed of me?"

"No, of course not. I can't believe you would be interested in me. I just think we should wait I don't want Dad putting you off."

"OK, I understand but I will ask you now, will you be my girl, Chrissy? I'll give you a good time take you to the best places buy you the things you need we can have a good life. I won't lie, I've had girlfriends in the past but you're different than them."

"Jimmy, just to be your girl is enough for me, I don't need to be taken to the best places nor am I interested in material things. When you walked out of my life six years ago, I thought I would never see you again, so I'm just happy to be Jimmy Cartwright's girl."

When Chrissy got home, she felt like she was walking on air, she touched her lips remembering his kisses, she was glad her parents were in bed because they would have guessed their daughter was in love.

As Jimmy drove home, his thoughts were on Chrissy. As his wipers swished backwards and forwards pushing the rain from his windscreen, he smiled. She has a warmth and generosity about her that was missing in his past girlfriends, she would make a good wife in the future. He frowned then smiled, yes why not? Maybe in a couple of years, he would like to settle down have a family. With that thought in mind, he began humming one of his favourite Tony Bennett songs *The good life.*

# Chapter 6

1<sup>st</sup> March, Iron Door Club, Liverpool

Jimmy and Chrissy were enjoying themselves at the Iron Door Club in Temple Street. There was a good line up on; The Undertakers, Sonny Webb and the Crusaders then Rory Storm and the Hurricanes. The atmosphere was buzzing and friendly and Chrissy was sipping a gin and tonic with ice which Jimmy had introduced to her. He was as usual smartly dressed in a white shirt a dark blue tie, a black sweater vest and grey trousers he had had his hair cut into the Beatles style. They had been dancing most of the night and were now sitting down having a rest. Jimmy seemed to be popular and well-known here and had introduced Chrissy to many people, another person he knew approached their table. "Hi Jimmy, long time no see how are yer doing, mate?"

Jimmy jumped up smiling and shook the man by the hand.

"Tony, it's great to see yer, mate. Where have yer been?"

"Aren't you going to introduce us Jimmy?" He was looking at Chrissy.

"Sorry. Tony this is Chrissy, Chrissy meet Tony, my best mate."

"Hi Chrissy." He took her hand and kissed it

She pulled her hand away.

"Take no notice of him. He thinks he is some sort of Romeo. Are you with someone, Tony?"

"Yea, she is over there. Can we join you and Chrissy?"

"Yea of course. You don't mind, do you love?"

"No, of course not." Although privately, she did mind, she wasn't too sure about Tony.

He came over with a woman who looked a lot older than him, she was a bottle blonde with her dark roots showing, she was wearing plenty of make-up with a bright red lipstick, she wore a short black skirt and a low-cut scarlet red low-cut blouse showing off her ample breasts. Tony wasn't as good looking as

Jimmy with his ebony black hair combed back, swarthy complexion and almost black eyes, he could still do better than her. Tony introduced her as Eileen and she sat down next to Chrissy, she noticed Eileen's long thin nicotine-stained fingers her nails were long and painted red close up she looked about forty.

"Hi Chrissy, nice to meet you. How long have you known Jimmy?"

"Two weeks." Chrissy didn't really want to get into a conversation with Eileen, they had nothing to talk about she looked a tart.

"Excuse me ladies while I nip to the gents." Tony followed Jimmy and left Chrissy alone with Eileen.

"Where have you been?" Jimmy asked, "haven't seen you around for ages."

"I went to London for a short time see if I could get something going there, money lending or protection but the Kray brothers have everything tied up. I heard what they do to any opposition, so I gave up and now I'm back. Are you still with the toad Gaffa Goff? I heard you were working for him."

"I am. It's steady work and I earn good money even though I hate the slimy get."

"Why don't you start up your own money lending I…" They stopped talking because someone had entered the gents and gave them a funny look.

"We can't talk here," whispered Jimmy. "Come to mine tomorrow. You know where we live now?"

"Yea, in Walton I heard. I'll be there about one is that OK?"

"Fine, let's get back to the girls. By the way, why are you with her? She looks a bit old for you."

"Eileen is 38, her hubby is in the navy, she knows how to give a guy a good time." He gave a wink.

They returned to the table and Jimmy could see Chrissy wasn't happy being left with Eileen so took her hand and led her to the dancefloor. *Unforgettable* was being sung and Jimmy took her in his arms and whispered, "Sorry I was so long, love. Tony kept me talking, we haven't seen each other for ages."

Chrissy forgot her bad mood and got lost in the magic of the song and being held in his arms. They never spoke while they danced and stayed in each other's arms when the song finished. When they returned to the table, Tony and Eileen were getting ready to leave.

Tony took Chrissy's hand and kissed it once more. "Goodnight you two. I'll see you tomorrow, Jimmy."

Eileen frowned then smiled at Chrissy. "Nice to have met you Chrissy, we might meet again." The smile did not reach her eyes Chrissy hoped she would never meet her again.

When they had left, Jimmy told her they would have to hurry and finish their drinks because it was now 11:15 and he didn't want to get into her dad's bad books by getting her home too late. Chrissy asked him about Tony. "I have known him and his family since I was a kid. He went to All Saints School. His parents are Italian, but Tony was born here in Liverpool. During the war, his dad was put into an internment camp on the Isle of Man, Antonio then decided to join the British army and fought against his own country, the people who had turned against the family changed their minds and made them their friends. My mum and his are the best of friends, although they still live in Breck Road they still visit each other. Antonio died while we were in London, that's one of the reasons Mum wanted to return to Liverpool."

Chrissy had thought Tony had looked foreign. He was good looking, but for some unknown reason she didn't trust him. She was sorry he had come into their lives but he was Jimmy's friend and she had to accept that.

They parked up in a side street off Scotland Road, there were hardly any houses left just piles of rubble. They were kissing and Chrissy couldn't stop the sensations that were coursing through her body, he had his hand inside her dress and was slowly caressing her breasts, she broke away.

He was breathless his voice rasping with passion he murmured, "Oh Chrissy, what's the matter? I thought you were enjoying it?"

"I am but things are getting too far forward. I have only known you for two weeks I have never let a boy touch me like that before."

"Sorry Chrissy, I can't help it. You're so gorgeous. Look, it's about time you told your family about me. I don't like this sneaking around. Your Norm has introduced Jean, I think you're ashamed of me."

Chrissy could just see his face in the pale light from the moon he looked sad.

"I can ask if you could come for tea on Sunday."

He smiled. "That would be great. I will meet you tomorrow at five, but I won't be able to take you out we can just go for a walk somewhere if the weather is fine." He looked at his watch. "Come on, I have 10 minutes to get you home."

As Chrissy walked to her house, she straightened her clothes and hair she didn't want her parents to see her like this if they were still up. It was getting harder to keep Jimmy at arm's length now he was so passionate and persuasive, she was not looking forward to telling her parents about Jimmy, it was only still two weeks she had really known him, and she still didn't know that much about him but she knew without a doubt that she loved him and hoped she could keep him interested because she wasn't really sure how he felt about her.

Chrissy could not sit still she was up and down the stairs in and out of the kitchen fussing over the slightest thing.

"Chrissy," her dad said. "Keep still, you're making me dizzy."

"Sorry Dad, sorry Mum. I just want to make sure everything is OK I just hope you both like him."

"If our Norm likes him and tells us he is a good bloke I trust his judgement," her dad replied.

At that moment, there was a knock on the door Chrissy just stood frozen. "Well, aren't you going to let the lad in?" Her parents laughed.

Chrissy had already told her parents all about Jimmy, where he lived and worked and that he owned a car, which impressed her brother Gerry. After all the introductions, Jimmy gave her mum flowers, her dad cigarettes and Gerry a bag of coloured marbles which had lit up his eyes.

"Thank you so much, Jimmy. The flowers are lovely."

"You didn't need to bribe us, son," her dad laughed.

Jimmy blushed. "Oh, I wasn't trying to do that, Mr Bennett."

"I was only joking, son." Her dad clapped him on the shoulder.

Chrissy noticed he had a box with a handle on.

He noticed her looking and smiled. "This is for you."

She took it and placed it on the table it had a lid on with a silver latch, she opened the latch and lifted the lid and gasped. "Oh Mum, Dad, it's a record player! I have been saving for ages but never seemed to have enough."

Jimmy told her it was a Danette Viva with autochanger which meant it could hold up to six single records which dropped one at a time and you could play LP's as well. "You will be able to play the ones I gave you now."

Her dad asked what records they were. Chrissy told him and then he turned to Jimmy, "That's a bit expensive. I don't think you have known each other long enough to be buying presents like that."

Chrissy's face dropped, trust her dad to spoil it, but Jimmy put his mind at ease.

"I didn't buy it, Mr Bennett. It belonged to my cousin who has emigrated, he gave it me I already had one, so it's been lying in the cupboard."

"It looks new to me," her dad replied.

"It's not that old but he couldn't take it because they have a different electricity power to ours."

"OK then, you can have it but no playing it too loud. Thank you, Jimmy."

"Come on, Chrissy. Get it off the table so we can have our tea come and give us a hand." Chrissy did as her mum asked and smiled over at Jimmy and he winked.

After a tea of corned beef salad with beetroot and cakes and biscuits, Gerry asked Jimmy if he could have a ride in his car. His mum told him not to be cheeky.

"It's OK, Mrs Bennett. I will give him a ride when I get another car."

Chrissy was surprised. "I didn't know you were changing your car what are you getting?"

"I'm not sure yet, but it will be bigger than the one I have now."

"Great! Can I have a ride then, Jimmy?"

"Of course, Gerry. We will take you to Southport in the summer."

Later, Chrissy asked her parents if she and Jimmy could use the front parlour to play records, the parlour was kept for best they mostly used the kitchen and another room at the back where the telly was housed. Her dad looked at his watch, it was eight.

"OK, but only till 9:30. It's work tomorrow and I will be retiring to bed keep it quiet."

"Thank you, Mr Bennett. It's not the kind of music you play loud. I will respect your wishes."

In the parlour, Jimmy put on the Tony Bennett LP *I wanna be around* they sat on the black leatherette settee and listened to the rich dulcet tones of the American singer as they listened to T*he good life* one of the songs on the LP. Jimmy pulled her to him and told her that's what they would have if she stuck with him.

Chrissy replied, "I told you I'm not bothered about material possessions. As long as we have each other, that's enough for me."

"Love is not enough, Chrissy. It won't feed you or cloth you or get you the best things in life. I want to give you those even take you to New York one day."

They kissed. *It* was a long deep kiss which left them both breathless Jimmy whispered. "Do you like the music? It's different, isn't it? Wait till you hear Etta James."

Chrissy was surprised that she did like the music she never thought she would, but Tony Bennetts voice melted her heart.

As Jimmy drove home, he thought about what he was going to take on, his meeting with Tony yesterday was interesting he wanted Jimmy to leave the employ of Gaffer Goff and go into partnership with him for their own money lending scheme. Jimmy was sceptical at first, he didn't want to cross Goff he was a dangerous volatile character, but Tony told him if they did a different area and take on new customers, they shouldn't get any trouble from Goff and his cronies. Jimmy asked his dad's advice because he needed his experience and help with funding. Albert Cartwright had his fingers in different schemes; he was a hard man but fair. He was also respected on the docks as a hard worker. After an afternoon of drinking and discussing the pros and cons, Jimmy decided to split from Goff with help from Tony and his dad. The only problem now was picking the right moment to tell Goff of his plans.

That Sunday, Norm and Jean had gone to see Summer Holiday with Cliff Richard and The Shadows, but Jean wasn't really concentrating on the film she was bored, Norm was a nice guy he wasn't like other guys she had gone out with he wasn't only interested in getting her to have sex. In fact, it was he who stopped if their petting was going too far. He told her he would wait till they were married because he respected her, if only he knew she was no virgin, marriage? Did she really want to settle down she was 21 now and up to now he was the only one who had mentioned marriage. But what would it entail marrying him? Would he be enough to keep her happy, he was a quiet serious man. She needed excitement. Now, if it was Jimmy Cartwright, that would be different. He was exciting, handsome and seemed to have plenty of money and he also had a car. Chrissy didn't realise how lucky she was having him as a boyfriend. The film ended. Norm asked if she wanted a drink before he took her home.

"I don't think I will. Tonight I feel like an early night."

"Oh, OK. Are you alright, love? You seem a bit quiet tonight."

"Just a bit tired, that all."

They jumped on the bus to Bootle and reached her flat where she lived with her mum and sister on the ground floor of a big house. Norman took her in his arms and kissed her. Oh how she excited him, he did want her what man wouldn't. But he would wait, next week he would propose to her.

"Goodnight, love. I will see you next week. I will book a table in a nice restaurant and have a meal for a change."

"Goodnight, Norm. I will look forward to that."

After work on the Monday, Chrissy went to see her friend May. She hadn't seen her for a few days and felt guilty. Mrs Makin opened the door; she was the same age as her mum but looked older because of her weight; she had a round face with kind big blue eyes she was small and well-rounded with big arms that made you feel safe when she hugged you. She smiled and welcomed her in.

"May!" she shouted up the stairs. "Chrissy has come to see you."

May came down the stairs smiling glad to see her friend.

"May, I feel I am neglecting you since I have been seeing Jimmy."

"Of course, you want to see Jimmy, don't worry about me."

Chrissy could see her friend was excited her eyes were twinkling, "Mum, do you mind if we take our tea upstairs?"

"Not yet," Chrissy replied. "I have only just arrived it seems a bit rude to abandon your mum."

Mrs Makin laughed, "I don't mind, pet. I know you girls want some privacy. Don't forget I was a teenager once."

When they were sitting on May's bed. May told her she had a boyfriend who she had gone out with twice. She told Chrissy he worked in Littlewoods where she worked, and they had said hello on a few occasions till he had plucked up courage to ask her out.

"His name is Gary and he is 25 and he lives in Aigburth."

She went on to tell Chrissy how he was well educated and was already an assistant manager of the finance department. "His father is a doctor in Rodney Street and his mother used to be a nurse, he also has a younger brother at university."

Chrissy listened to Chrissy praise Gary and his family and wondered if her friend was captivated by the idea of his family.

"Chrissy, he is so sweet and good looking, he is not a bit conceited because he has been to university. I feel so comfortable in his company."

Chrissy was surprised but happy for her friend that she had met someone she need not feel guilty for abandoning her to be with Jimmy.

"Why don't we go out as a foursome?" asked May. "We would love to go to those clubs you visit because Gary isn't fussy on pop music like your Jimmy."

Chrissy wasn't sure if he would like the places they went to and wasn't even sure if Jimmy and Gary would like each other but decided she would ask him anyway.

"OK. I will ring his house and ask him about this Friday, we are going to the Mardi Gras to see the Mississippi."

After she left her friend, Chrissy decided to ring Jimmy to ask about Friday, the phone was answered by his mum. "Sorry, love, he is out with his dad. I don't know what time they will be back; I will pass on your message and ask him to call you back."

At that moment, Jimmy with his dad and Tony were in the Grove Inn. Jimmy had gone to the back room to speak to Goff, his dad, Tony and two friends stayed in the bar to keep their eyes on the door and stop any trouble. Goff looked up when Jimmy entered Goff had his minders either side of him. "I wasn't expecting you today, what's up?"

Jimmy felt nervous but he couldn't let Goff and minders see his nerves. "I have come to tell you I'm leaving your scheme, Goff."

There was silence, Goff stared at Jimmy turned to his minders and smirked then turned back to Jimmy with a frown on his fat face.

"What do you mean you're leaving Cartwright?" he shouted and hit the table with his fist. "You don't tell me when you leave, I tell you."

His minders moved from his side and made towards Jimmy, but Goff told them to stay. Jimmy took his courage in both hands and calmly told Goff he was setting up his own lending scheme but in a different area and with new clients it wouldn't interfere with Goff's turf. Goff asked who he was setting up with his piggy eyes staring at him with malice. "No one you know, Goff." He didn't want to name his dad or Tony yet.

Goff was silent he picked up his drink and slowly drank the pint leaving froth around his loose sloppy mouth he wiped his mouth with the back of his hand then threw the empty glass at Jimmy. Luckily for him, he was quick enough to jump out of the way and the glass smashed against the door, at that moment the door was flung open and his dad, Tony and their two friends ran into the room. Goff ran behind one of the minders while the other ran at Tony, the smaller of the intruders, one of their friends who was as big and muscle bound as the minder punched him on the chin which left the minder staggering backwards and falling onto the bare floorboards. Jimmy told Goff he didn't want to fight with him he just wanted an amical parting of their ways. Goff sat down and looked at his minder on the floor.

"OK Cartwright, you can fuck off and if ever you come near here or encroach on my clients, you had better watch your back."

Albert Cartwright went to the table leaned towards Goff and staring him in the face told him, "If you or any of your cronies ever lay a finger on him or my friends, it will be you lying on the floor, but you will never get back up."

They left Goff who was shaking with anger, he turned to his minder. "Get him off the floor, you fool." He wasn't going to let Cartwright get away with this, no one was going to make Gaffer Goff look a fool no one, he would bide his time, but he would get revenge on the Cartwrights.

# Chapter 7

Jimmy, his dad, Tony and their two friends left the Grove Inn and walked towards Scotland Road they had decided to have a few drinks.

Jimmy told his dad, "Good job you arrived in time. I knew he would be angry but not that bad we will have to watch our backs for a while."

"He has his minders we will have ours," Albert replied. "How many clients have you lined up, Tony?"

"Word has got around Jimmy is setting up his own money lending scheme and Mary has told her friends. So far we have 10."

"We need more to make it worthwhile for all of us to make money. Leave the minders for now dad."

They entered the Throstles Nest the air was thick with cigarette smoke, they ordered pints of bitter and whisky chasers. Jimmy looked around the bar which was busy he knew some of the drinkers and nodded to them, his dad knew a few from the docks he went over to speak to them. Jimmy noticed Nosey Jones and Roachy who acknowledged him, his dad was in deep conversation with two men who Jimmy hadn't seen before, he took a long swig of his pint and saw his dad walking back. "Who were they?" he asked his dad. "Oh, lads from the Seaforth side. They have a shipment due in full of whisky and cigarettes. I won't go into any further details yet son too many here with big ears and big mouths."

That night, they did a pub crawl they visited the Pen and Wig, the Parrott then the Royal on Stanley Road, the group now happily drunk split up and went their separate ways.

Jimmy, Chrissy, May and Gary met at the Mardi Gras, after introductions they found a table and Jimmy and Gary went to the bar.

"Well?" May asked. "What do you think of Gary?"

"I like him, he seems a decent bloke. He doesn't brag about his family or that he has a degree. Have you met his parents yet?"

"I'm going for tea on Sunday. I hope I don't make a show of myself."

"I'm sure you won't. Just be yourself, you're a lovely kind girl I'm sure they will love you."

Jimmy and Gary seemed to like each other and chatted easily they talked about music, cars and politics. Jimmy told him and Chrissy he was getting another car. "It's a Ford Consul classic four door saloon in blue only a year old and was just the right size." Chrissy was pleased the car he had now was so cramped, but she did wonder how he could afford a new car.

After an enjoyable evening, they bade goodnight to May and Gary, Chrissy climbed into Jimmy's two-seater.

"I'm glad you're getting a bigger car. I don't want to pry but, can you afford a new car?"

"I'm OK. I have earned more commission so I can afford it," he replied with an edge of annoyance to his voice.

Chrissy detected this and told herself to mind her own business.

"I'm sorry, Jimmy. I'm nosy, aren't I?"

Jimmy laughed and told her yes and squeezed her leg, he parked up and turned to her.

"It will be better with the new car; it has more room and seats at the back where we will be more comfortable for kissing and cuddling." He had a glint in his dark brown eyes and a smile on his lips.

"Trust you to think of that," Chrissy laughed.

They kissed and Chrissy had to stop Jimmy from going further she didn't know how long she keep saying no to his advances she was afraid he might get fed up and leave her but she also felt if she gave in to his advances, he might still leave her, as yet he had promised them being together promising her a good life and taking her to New York but he hadn't told her he loved her.

Her thoughts came to an end as he took her in his arms once again and kissed her.

"I do love you, Jimmy," she whispered breathing heavily.

"Why don't you show me then, Chrissy. I want to show you how much I love you." His voice heavy with passion

"Do you love me, Jimmy? Because if you do, you will wait."

Jimmy never usually saw Chrissy during the week because he was busy but today Monday. he needed to say sorry for the way he behaved on the Saturday, he knocked on her door and her mum answered.

"I hope I haven't called at the wrong time, Mrs Bennett, but would it be possible to see Chrissy?"

"Of course, Jimmy come on in she is in the back washing the dishes."

Chrissy entered the living room when she heard his voice and smiled.

"I thought I heard your voice. You don't usually call on a Monday, is everything alright?"

"Can we go out for a walk somewhere? You can see my new car as well, I picked it up this afternoon."

At the mention of the new car, Gerry got up from the floor where he had been playing with his marbles.

"Can I have a ride, Jimmy?"

"Not yet Gerry, but I will let you have a look now and get in it for a bit."

Mrs Bennett chided her son. "I told you our Gerry, don't be so cheeky Jimmy wants to take your sister out."

"I don't mind," replied Jimmy ruffling Gerry's hair.

"He can look while I get a quick change," Chrissy told her brother and gave him a wink.

Later, while walking in Sefton Park the trees were still bare but had the signs of new buds, there was still a hint of the cold March breeze with a pale sun trying to warm the early evening it would soon be spring, and the clocks would be going forward making the days longer. Chrissy was deep in thought she didn't normally see Jimmy during the week, and he seemed to have something on his mind was he trying to tell her they were over. Jimmy broke the silence and led her to a park bench and took her hand in his.

"I'm sorry about Saturday. I was a bit edgy with you and I misbehaved I do respect you and shouldn't demand sex from you. I do love you Chrissy you're different from any girl I have seen before who have let me have my way after a couple of dates, but they are not the ones I want to marry your fun to be with and gorgeous, so don't think I don't care for you."

Chrissy was speechless she didn't expect him to say he wanted to marry her if that's what he meant.

"Does that mean you want to marry me?"

"Yes, I do. I have known for ages that you were the one for me but; last Saturday I realised I didn't want to risk losing you."

"No chance of that Jimmy, because I have loved you from the moment, we met six years ago."

40

"Come on, let's go for a drink and talk some more it's getting chilly now."

The March breeze was a lot brisker now and the branches were bending slightly on the bare trees, they found a pub with an open blazing fire and sat at the table with their drinks. Jimmy told her his parents were giving him a 21st birthday in July.

"I will ask your parents if we can get engaged and make it a double celebration, we can get married next year. On Saturday, we can go to Chester buy you a ring then go for a meal."

"Oh yes, can we go home now and ask them?"

"We will. The sooner the better."

They had returned to Chrissy's and Jimmy had asked if they could get engaged and were disappointed when her dad had said no.

"Why not dad? We love each other it's not as if I have a career to think about."

"I still think it's too soon. Nothing against you Jimmy, but you have only been going out together for four weeks, have time to know each other properly first why the rush? You're not in trouble, are you, my girl?"

Chrissy blushed and her mother scolded her father.

"Norman, how dare you think our daughter is like that! You should be ashamed of yourself."

Her dad had the decency to hang his head and apologise to Chrissy.

"I'm sorry, love. I should know you're not that kind of girl."

Chrissy was upset. "Mum, Dad, we are only getting engaged we won't be getting married till next year."

"You're only 18, why do you want to tie yourself down?" her dad responded.

"I'm old enough to know that I love Jimmy and there won't be anyone else."

Jimmy decided to speak. "I can understand your doubts, Mr Bennett, but I can assure you that I love and respect your daughter. I am able to keep her and give her the life she deserves. I will look after her and care for her the way you and Mrs Bennett have, you have done a marvellous job and should be proud."

Norman liked the lad he had spoken well which proved he did love Chrissy.

"Me and your mum will go into the front parlour and discuss this. Chrissy, you make a pot of tea then we will let you know over a cup of tea."

After a nerve jangling ten minutes, her parents returned their faces were serious, Chrissy and Jimmy thought they were going to say no.

41

"OK, you have our permission, but we ask you to wait longer before you get wed."

Chrissy ran into her dad's arms and kissed him on the cheek. "Oh, Dad thank you thank you."

Jimmy shook her dad by the hand while Chrissy was hugged by her mum, then Jimmy pecked her on the cheek.

"Thank you, Mr Bennett, Mrs Bennett."

"Now you are engaged to our daughter, I think it's time you started calling us by our first names, Jimmy."

They were all busy talking and drinking tea when Chrissy's brother Norm walked in.

"What's all the noise about? What's happened?"

After telling him, there were more hugs and handshakes.

"I think it's time this little celebration came to an end, its work tomorrow."

Chrissy stepped outside with Jimmy.

"I don't think I will sleep tonight, I'm that excited."

"I don't think I will either," he laughed. They kissed goodnight and Jimmy made his way home.

Jimmy felt a bit guilty he had not yet told Chrissy the truth about his money lending, he knew she wouldn't like what he did and the people he knew so he decided to keep it to himself till they were married. His dad had discussed with him the load of tobacco and spirits that were due into Seaforth docks, he knew a security guard who told him the times the delivery were due and when he would be on duty, all they had to do was rough him up a bit tie him to make it look good, this was to be carried out in the early hours of the morning load into a stolen van drive to Wales then get the Irish ferry to offload the stuff to a contact Albert knew in Ireland. Jimmy wasn't sure if they should go down that road of robbing, but his dad told him till the money lending scheme brought in more money this would keep them going. Jimmy had finally given in after his dad reassured him there would be no violence involved. The heist would be carried out by Albert, Tony, Ritchie and Billy their friends. Jimmy would carry out his usual routine of collecting the loan money. It was due to be carried out on the Friday morning, Jimmy hoped there would be no complications, and everything would run smoothly, it was decided that Albert would not go to Ireland but to go into work as normal on the Friday.

# Chapter 8

## Seaforth Dock

It was 2 a.m. and the group were at the dock waiting in the van, they watched a man open the gates to the warehouse, but instead of waiting for them to enter the guard began to close them, the group looked at each other bewildered. What was he doing? Tony decided to speed towards the closing gates. As the van drew near, the guard shouted and jumped from the path of the speeding van, it came to a screeching halt the tyres leaving skid marks on the gravel, the occupants jumped out and ran towards the guard. Albert then realised it was a different guard. As he ran towards to the office, Tony chased him while the others went to load the van thinking Tony could deal with the guard. When Tony caught up with him, the guard had just picked up the phone to call the police a scuffle broke out when Tony snatched the phone leaving the phone and papers to fall to the floor. As Tony fought with the guard, Albert and the others were loading the van they had managed to load a good amount when they heard a shot ring out into the silent night.

"Bloody hell!" shouted Billy. "What's happened?" They ran to the office and saw the guard on the floor with blood covering his coat. Tony stood with a gun in his hand.

"How did this happen?" Albert shouted. "Why did you bring a gun?"

Tony came out of his trance and told him he had pulled the gun on the guard but during the scuffle the gun had gone off.

"You stupid bloody fool! Get in the van, but first throw that into the dock before. I have the urge to throw you in."

The group then drove off into the night leaving the guard bleeding on the office floor.

Albert arrived home at 4 a.m. He was cold inside maybe it was shock after what had happened, he poured himself a drink from a couple of bottles he had taken from the dock. It was not worth going to bed so he lit the gas fire and put a blanket over his shoulders and decided to sleep on the settee, he hoped his wife would wake him when she got up to make his breakfast. Albert was 48 and still in his prime he had a full head of dark brown hair showing no signs of greying, he was slightly smaller than his son but broader in the chest he was still a good-looking man but in a different way too his son who had perfect features like his beloved wife. After a fitful sleep, Albert woke suddenly with a mist in front of him his head also felt heavy he was being shaken by his wife. "Wake up, love. Why were you on the settee? You should have come to bed."

Albert slowly came to he hadn't slept well and had had a dream about someone getting shot. Then it came to him like a bolt from the blue there had been a shooting the guard might be dead he felt sick he then noticed a bottle of whisky with the contents nearly empty.

"Shall I cook you some sausages as well as the bacon and eggs, love?"

"No thanks, can I have two rounds of toast and a cup of strong coffee?"

After his small breakfast and a wash, Albert was ready for work, he asked his wife if Jimmy was still in bed.

"I could do with a lift into work, I'm running late."

"Are you alright, Albert? You don't look too well. Your very pale and your sweating was it wise to stay out so late and drink that much?"

"Don't go on, love. I will be OK once I get going go and wake our Jimmy up."

Jimmy was still half asleep as he drove his dad to work, he had had a late night, but he needed to know how the robbery went and why his dad looked so terrible he had a horrible feeling that something had happened.

"How did it go, Dad?"

"Bad, son. Very bad. We managed to get the van loaded but it was a different guard there was a scuffle and Tony had brought a gun and shot him in the stomach it was an accident."

Jimmy stopped the car and turned to his dad in shock.

"Why did he bring a bloody gun! I told him no violence, what happened to the other guard?"

"I don't know, don't you be shouting at me show some respect. Don't you think I'm bloody shocked and shit scared I saw the fella lying there bleeding, it's no use us arguing we will find out later whether he survived it might be in the Echo later, the lads told me they would ring me later at the telephone box in

44

County Road. I don't want to risk them phoning the house, when they get home from Ireland, we will have a few words to say to Tony, I told him to dump the gun in the dock."

It was front page news in the Liverpool Echo that evening:

## VIOLENT ROBBERY AT SEAFORTH DOCKS

The article went on to tell its readers that a guard who had been relieving the original guard due to illness had been found lying on the office floor with a gunshot wound to his abdomen. There had obviously been a struggle because of objects strewn across the floor including the telephone, the guard had been found by the guards reporting for morning duty they had been surprised to see the warehouse doors open. The guard had unfortunately died of his injuries due to the amount of time he had lay undiscovered, the police would not be disclosing the guard's identity till further enquiries were carried out and his family had been informed.

Albert put the paper down and poured himself another whisky.

"The poor sod he should not have been on duty that night." He heard that the guard who Albert knew was being questioned by the police. He hoped he would keep his mouth shut he couldn't risk seeing him yet to ask if he had deliberately went off sick that night. He looked at his watch time he went to the telephone box.

"Just nipping out for a while, love. Won't be long then we can go out."

Gladys picked up the glass from the table and looked at the whisky bottle, she frowned the robbery at the dock was whisky and cigarettes she hoped her Albert was not involved in this because a man had died she knew Albert had little schemes going nothing big just little extras to give them the nicer things in life like the modern furniture the bathroom they had she didn't mind but robbery with violence that was another matter.

That evening in the Bennett household Norman had just finished reading the Echo and was shaking his head.

"I don't know what's happening, someone getting shot in our city it's becoming like America."

"Oh, don't be so dramatic, love. It's not that bad it hardly ever happens here."

"Cor, Gerry proclaimed it's like those gangster movies it's exciting."

Norman put down the paper. "It's not exciting, Gerard! It's murder. Some poor innocent man has lost his life because some people got greedy and decided to steal stuff that wasn't theirs, that guard might have been married had a family maybe a son your age how do you think they are going to feel now would you like it if I got shot?"

Gerry looked at his dad who hardly ever shouted at him, he didn't normally cry that was for sissies, but this time he could not stop the tears from falling the thought of his dad getting shot scared him.

Madge came in from the kitchen when she heard her husband shouting at Gerry and saw that he was crying.

"Ok, father you have made your point quite clear you have scared him and made him cry hope your happy now."

Norman admitted he had gone too far and put his arm around his son. "Sorry Gerry but I don't want you thinking that shooting anyone is exciting."

Chrissy came in from visiting her friend May to get ready to meet Jimmy they were only going the pub tonight for drinks with his parents so they could get to know her better, she noticed a tense atmosphere Gerry was lying on the floor reading the Beano comic, her mum was watching the television and her dad was reading the sports page of the Echo.

"I'm just going upstairs to get changed Jimmy will be here soon is our Norm in yet?"

Her mum answered. "OK love he is getting ready to meet Jean." Her dad had not even acknowledged her, she met her brother on the landing he was dressed in a grey sleeveless jumper with a white shirt a black leather jacket and grey flannels, he was growing a moustache which made him look older.

"Have Mum and Dad argued?"

"Dad upset Gerry by shouting at him," Norm went on to tell Chrissy about the newspaper headlines and Gerry's reaction about gangsters and their dad telling him off. Chrissy had read the paper and was shocked that anything like that could happen in Liverpool. Her brother just shrugged. "It's not the first time its happened don't suppose it will be the last if none of our family or friends get involved in criminal activity it should not affect us don't worry sis."

Chrissy went into her room to get changed she decided to wear a polo neck sweater in pale pink and a pair of black bell bottom trousers which were popular. She heard a knock on the door and ran down to meet Jimmy.

Later, Chrissy, Jimmy and his parents were having a drink in the County Pub on County Road Walton, the Beatles song *Love me do* was playing on the juke box and people were singing along, the atmosphere was friendly it was a Friday night most had been paid and it was the weekend. Chrissy and Gladys were also singing along she liked his mum, she was of small stature and was very attractive, although Jimmy had dark eyes and hair, he was more like his mum in looks. She was younger than her own mum not yet forty light blue eyes and blond hair which she wore loose. She was also modern in her outlook and enjoyed pop music she was so easy to talk to. They were both drinking gin and tonics while the men were drinking pints of bitter, Jimmy and his dad were deep in conversation and looking serious Chrissy wondered what was wrong. Gladys noticed Chrissy looking at them and frowning and thought they were spoiling their night out. Jimmy went to the bar and Chrissy the toilet while they were alone Gladys asked her husband. "Why all the whispering the both of you are spoiling the night for us talk to us not between yourselves its rude leave your business for another time."

She got up and sat by her husband so that Jimmy could sit by Chrissy. Albert went to the bar to help Jimmy with the drinks and told him to leave their problems for tonight and take more notice of their wife and girlfriend. Jimmy sat by Chrissy and put his arm around her shoulder. "Sorry if I neglected you, let's enjoy tonight." He then kissed her.

Albert followed suit and kissed his wife. They all had a great time that night singing and dancing to the music.

Albert, Jimmy, Tony, Ritchie and Billy were in Tony's flat, it consisted of a two-bar electric fire a brown plastic settee which had seen better days, a cooker in one corner which was covered in grease a cupboard and a single iron bedstead. In the middle of the room stood a Formica-topped table with three chairs, Tony was sitting on the settee warming his hands by the fire.

"Bloody hell," Albert exclaimed looking around, "you can afford better than this dump now why didn't you stay at your mam's?"

Tony gave a wicked smile, "how can I entertain my lady friends at my mam's?"

"I'm surprised you're not ashamed to bring them here no wonder you can't keep a girl," Jimmy laughed.

"I don't want a steady girl, yet I want to play around before I settle down, they don't call me Tony the Romeo for nothing yer know."

Albert called a halt to the light-hearted banter, "Ok, let's get down to business sorry Tony but the sooner I get out of here the better, now put the money from the haul on the table so we can share it out then go."

They had managed to sell the whisky and cigarettes and under instructions from Albert dumped the van and burnt it.

"Have you seen that guard yet?" asked Billy.

"No, I don't want to risk it till the cops are satisfied he wasn't in on the robbery, I will keep his share for…" He held his hand up as Billy was going to protest.

"I know he wasn't part of it but it was him who tipped me off and I want to keep him happy and to keep his mouth shut."

They picked their share from the table and Albert told them to be careful. "Don't go mad splashing the cash yet it will arouse suspicion."

"You're taking your Mrs on holiday," Tony argued.

"I know but I booked that holiday well before its only Cornwall not Spain just you be careful Tony and you won't be bringing any weapons with you anymore do you understand if it wasn't for the fact, I know your mam you would have got a bloody beating from me, did you throw that gun in the dock?"

"Yes," Tony replied even though it was a lie.

# Chapter 9

4<sup>th</sup> July 1963

## Aigburth Peoples Hall

Chrissy and her family and friends were gathered to celebrate Jimmy's 21<sup>st</sup> birthday. The hall had been suggested by Gary her friend May's boyfriend who lived in Aigburth with his parents and told Jimmy it would be perfect. It held up-to one hundred and fifty people had two bars and was close to Sefton Park and not far from Liverpool City centre. The table around the edge of the room were laden with plenty of food which consisted of ham sandwiches, chicken rolls, pork pies and fresh salmon, his parents had certainly pushed the boat out and why not he was their only child and they doted on him. The introductions had been carried out and everyone were enjoying themselves, they had a live band and they were belting out all the popular songs from the Beatles, Gerry and the pacemakers, the Merseybeat's and even some American artists, Elvis Presley and Bill Haley's *Rock around the clock* which most of the young ones enjoyed. Chrissy, Jimmy, May, Gary, Jean, Norm Arthur and his girlfriend Rose had just danced to *Let's twist again* by Chubby Checker, they had laughed trying to twist their bodies to the floor without falling to the floor.

Chrissy was asked to dance by Tony she didn't want to but didn't want to spoil the night by refusing him. He took her hand and pulled her onto the dancefloor he was a bit unsteady on his feet it was obvious he was drunk; the band were playing *Love me tender* by Elvis Presley. Tony pulled her into his arms his breath smelt strongly of alcohol and cigarettes he was breathing heavily and pushed himself against her, he could hardly dance and was just moving around in circles with his head leaning on her shoulder.

"Oh, Chrissy give ush a khiss, he slurred I fancy you have done shish I met yer."

"If Jimmy hears you talking like this to me, he will hit you friend or not let me go please before he notices anything is wrong."

She pushed him away and he bumped into Arthur. "OK, mate watch what yer doing are you alright Chrissy?"

"Yes, I'm fine Arthur just leave him he has had too much to drink no harm done."

She watched Tony stagger over to the woman he was with grab her hand and walk out. Chrissy looked around and saw Jimmy dancing with Jean it was obvious she was doing most of the talking while they danced. Later, the lights were dimmed, and his mum and dad walked over to Jimmy with a cake with 21 lit candles, the band played happy birthday while they all sang along while Jimmy blew them all out. His parents had organised a photographer who took lots of pictures of Jimmy with his family, friends, Chrissy's family them himself and Chrissy themselves, after the photos were taken before he sliced the cake Jimmy asked for silence.

"I would like to thank my mum and dad for giving me this party and the generous gift of forty pounds, I would also like to thank everyone for attending and for their card and gifts. I'm not just celebrating my birthday this is a double celebration I would like Chrissy to join me here on the stage."

Chrissy walked over and watched him pull out a box then a ring, he then got down on one knee and asked her if she would marry him, she didn't hesitate she answered yes, there was a big cheer and Jimmy hugged and kissed her. Chrissy knew about the ring they had gone to Chester in March to buy it but decided to wait till his party to announce their engagement, what surprised her was Jimmy getting down on one knee and proposing in front of their family and friends. Everyone wanted to look at her engagement ring which was a solitaire surrounded by little coloured diamonds on an eighteen-carat gold band.

Chrissy's and Jimmy's parents congratulated both of them, then Norm, Gary May and Tony who seemed sober shook Jimmy's hand and kissed Chrissy, Arthur stood behind them Chrissy turned and smiled while Rose pushed him forward to congratulate them. Jean went to the toilet, she felt insanely jealous and didn't want to see the ring.

The party carried on till one in the morning although some of the older relatives had left earlier. When they arrived at Chrissy's her parents who had left earlier to take Gerry home had gone to bed. They crept in and went into the front parlour and fell onto the settee giggling they both felt a little tipsy.

"Come here, future wife." Pulling her into his arms he kissed her hard on the lips then he moved down to her neck she responded with a strong desire and their kisses became deeper, Jimmy began to unbutton her dress then pulled it over her head he was just beginning to unfasten her bra when the light suddenly flashed on, they jumped apart and saw her mum standing in the doorway in her dressing gown.

"Come on you two I know you're engaged but that will have to wait it's a good job your dad didn't see you, I went into your room to see if you were home and noticed the hall light on, make yourself decent Chrissy and I think it's time you said goodnight, Jimmy and went home."

As Jimmy made his way home Madge warned her daughter to behave herself. "I know you love each other, and you can get carried away but if Jimmy has any respect for you, he will wait till you are married, go to bed I won't tell your dad."

Chrissy climbed the stairs went into her room got undressed and lay in bed but she could not sleep she remembered his kisses and how she felt, he had aroused a passion in her she had never thought she had, any longer and she would have given in to his lovemaking, she wasn't sure to thank her mum or curse her for stopping them going too far. As Jimmy went home, he too was feeling frustrated, trust her mum to come down then he knew for certain that Chrissy was ready to give in. He loved her and did respect her, but he was a man who had needs, he had had no problems in the past persuading women to let him make love. Tonight, as he danced with Jean, she had made it obvious she would welcome him into her bed, she had no shame. She had told him if Chrissy was anything like her brother when it came to premarital sex, she felt sorry for him and if he wanted to call at her flat next week while her mum and sister were away, he would be welcome. He had laughed it off and told her no chance he loved Chrissy, He now had second thoughts he might just take Jean up on her offer.

Norm was discussing his forthcoming 21$^{st}$ birthday celebrations with his mum and dad he was also celebrating finishing his apprenticeship and job offer at the Automatic. He kept to himself that he was also going to propose to Jean, she had no idea what he was planning. He had the intention of asking her months ago but lost his nerve, he knew he was lucky to have her as a girlfriend, she was gorgeous with her long thick auburn hair porcelain complexion big hazel eyes and voluptuous figure which she showed off with her tight blouses and jumpers she was every man's dream woman, she loved dancing and was always laughing she bought Norm out of his shell and he felt a different person when in her company. He just hoped she wanted to marry him as much as he wanted to marry her. His mum told him it wouldn't be as big and fancy as Jimmy's.

"Mum, don't worry I'm grateful you're giving me a party they only have one son so can afford to spoil him." He kissed his mum on the cheek.

"What's that for?" she laughed.

"For being my mum."

Chrissy came in from next door and was asked by her brother. "Are you seeing Jimmy tonight I want to ask him about that band he had, and would they be free in two weeks' time, I really liked them."

"Not tonight but I can ring him and ask."

"Will you ring him now just in case they are booked up I was going to have records, but I think they would be better the church hall is big enough."

"OK Norm I will go and ring him now."

She rang Jimmy's house and after a few rings his mum answered she told Chrissy that Jimmy was out but gave Chrissy the contact number of the group's singer. She then gave the number to her brother and wondered what Jimmy was doing this evening.

Jimmy was at that moment in Jean's flat having a drink and a kiss and a cuddle on her settee, Jean took Jimmy by the hand and led him into her bedroom.

Jimmy woke he looked at Jean who was asleep with her arms above her head her naked body glistening in the moonlight, he had enjoyed himself tonight she was a very sexy woman, but she wasn't Chrissy, he had a moment of guilt he did love Chrissy, but she wouldn't give him what he needed. He was just about to sneak out of bed and looked at the bedside clock it was midnight he had better go home. She stirred and turned to him and in a soft whisper asked if he was leaving her.

"Yes, I'll have to get home." And pecked her on her cheek.

"Please stay a little longer," she pleaded her hazel eyes had a hint of a tear.

Jimmy climbed back into bed where they made love once more.

Norm managed to book the band luckily, they had a cancellation. There wasn't as many people at his party because it was only a church hall, he had invited his work mates and their wives and girlfriends, his best mate Arthur and his girlfriend Rose, his aunts and uncles and of course Jean her mum and sister and Chrissy and Jimmy. Jimmy's parents were on holiday in Cornwall. There was good spread on, and they were having a good time. Jimmy was just hovering behind Arthur and two of Norms friends and they were discussing the robbery and shooting. Arthur, a police constable, was now answering questions about the shooting.

"I can't tell you any more than what you read in the paper its still being investigated."

"I heard you have seen the body before it was taken away," Norm asked.

"Yes, I did my sergeant told me to have a look to get used to it but that's all I can tell you otherwise I will be in trouble."

Trust him to be involved thought Jimmy he would have to be careful; he then heard his parents' names being mentioned Arthur asked Norm how a docker could afford to give Jimmy a big party in a posh hall and have fresh salmon. Jimmy walked up to them and shouted. "Not that it's any of your business but they have been saving for years for my 21st birthday."

Arthur had the grace to look embarrassed and Jimmy walked away Norm told Arthur, "Serves you right mate for questioning their privacy."

Later, Norm's dad asked for silence and told the partygoers how proud he was of his son, he then gave him an envelope which Norman opened and found twenty-five pounds inside. "That's from me your mum and Chrissy," his dad told him. His cake was then bought out with 21 candles which he blew out and they sang happy birthday. Norm then told everyone he hoped tonight would be a treble celebration he looked at Jimmy and told him he was sorry to copy him then took out a box then a ring, he went to Jean went down on one knee and asked her to marry him. Unlike Chrissy Jean hesitated, there was a silence Norm's hand shook as he held out the ring, after what seemed a long time to Norm Jean smiled and answered yes, he then placed the ring on her finger, of course it wasn't as big as Chrissy's, but it was nice. Jean looked over at Jimmy who was in deep conversation with Chrissy, so he did not see the look of jealousy in her eyes.

Jimmy was telling Chrissy what Arthur was saying about his parents he was angry she had not seen him like this before.

"He had no right questioning how my parents could pay for my party, they have worked hard to save to give me that."

"Come on let's go outside." Chrissy could see people looking at Jimmy she didn't want her brother's birthday spoiled.

Once outside the air was warm even though it was now half past ten, there were some of the party-goers standing outside getting some fresh air. She took Jimmy out of earshot and linked her arm through his.

"Jimmy take no notice of Arthur it's the way he is now always asking questions he has changed since joining the police."

"Yea, well he had better keep his mouth shut."

Chrissy was surprised by Jimmy's attitude he was usually easy going and laughed off criticism.

After a few moments of silence, he smiled and said. "Sorry love lets go in and enjoy the rest of the party."

She smiled back glad he had recovered from his bad mood, but she was worried for some unknown reason he had changed in the last couple of weeks and wondered if something was bothering him.

# Chapter 10

Tuesday 4<sup>th</sup> August

Jimmy had just taken Jean home they had been to New Brighton and spent the evening in a quiet location where he parked up. He had been seeing Jean once a week for the past four weeks. They had to go somewhere they were not seen, they would usually make out in the back of his car in a secluded spot. It was midnight and when he pulled up outside his home, he noticed the lights were on, he frowned his parents were usually in bed by now, he entered the house and walked into the kitchen and found his mum sitting at the table in her dressing gown and slippers drinking tea she looked up.

"Oh, it's you Jimmy, I thought it might have been your dad he is not home yet, he told me he wouldn't be late tonight he usually keeps his promise."

Jimmy sat down and took his mum's hand.

"Mum, you know what he is like he has most probably been asked to play cards and forgot the time."

"He would have phoned me he knows how I worry."

Jimmy was worried he knew his dad had gone to meet the security guard who had tipped him off about the delivery of tobacco and whisky, the police were now satisfied he had nothing to do with the robbery when he proved he had been unwell that night, Albert was giving him a cut of the money they had made.

"Mum, go to bed I will stay up and wait for him we can't do anything yet if he hasn't arrived by this morning, I will go around to his friends to ask if they have seen him, try and get some sleep."

Jimmy sat in the fireside chair then drifted off to sleep, he awoke with a start and looked at his watch it was now 6 a.m. and his dad hadn't returned he was due to leave for work soon, where was he? He heard his mum walking down the stairs he rubbed the sleep from his eyes and noticed her eyes were red and puffy.

"I'm going to check on his friends and ask if they saw him last night, I will ring you later to see if he has returned home, try not to worry."

He got a quick wash and was made to drink some coffee, neither of them wanted to eat, he then drove off to search for his dad.

Chrissy got ready for work unaware of the disappearance of Albert Cartwright, she was meeting Jimmy tonight and they were going to visit his Uncle Jack who lived in Crosby-Chrissy hoped he was in a better mood than Sunday, they had taken Gerry to Southport, he had eaten candy floss, fish and chips and drank lemonade, he then had some rides on the fairground, but on the way home he was sick in the car, Jimmy hadn't shouted at him but she could tell he wasn't pleased by the way his mouth was set in a thin line and the twinkle was no longer evident in his dark brown eyes. They had returned to Chrissy's when her mum had put Gerry to bed and she and Jimmy had cleaned the car, luckily Gerry hadn't been sick on the back seat but on the floor, it smelt a bit but it hadn't spoilt the car too much, Chrissy had gone to see how her brother was feeling but found him fast asleep. Later, they had gone out for a drink but he had wanted to go home early, he had parked up and asked her to get into the back seat for a kiss and cuddle Chrissy had willingly obliged and she had enjoyed his kisses till he had put his hand where she had felt uncomfortable he was lying on top of her, she had asked him to stop but he had moaned and told her he had protection it would be OK he was still trying to make love to her when she had used all her strength to push him back and managed to get out of the car, she had stood outside fixing her clothes while he had got back into the driver's seat and sat waiting for her, they drove home in silence and when they arrived at Chrissy's he had leaned over and kissed her on the cheek, before she got out the car she asked him if they were still alright he had smiled and told her of course we are he told her he was sorry about the way he had behaved and asked to see her on Tuesday.

Jimmy visited his dad's friends and they told him they had not seen him last night, he asked Tony, Ritchie and Billy who gave him the same answer. Jimmy was mystified just where was his dad, he had phoned home, but his dad had still not arrived his mum had sounded distraught, so he returned home. Gladys asked if she should call the police.

"I will ring the hospitals first to ask if a man had been admitted." He was just about to ring when there came a knock on the door, he answered it and found Arthur on the doorstep in his police uniform, Jimmy's stomach felt knotted.

"Can I come in Jimmy?"

He was friendly; Jimmy didn't like this he took him into the kitchen, when his mum saw Arthur, she screamed. "It's my Albert he's dead, isn't he?"

Arthur took his helmet off and stood by her side and patted her shoulder.

"No, Mrs Cartwright he is not dead but he is in hospital he was found badly beaten early this morning, he had no identification on him and was unconscious he also has a broken leg and arm so they had no idea who he was, but he has regained consciousness now and was able to tell the doctor who he was and where he lived, when they informed the police I told my sergeant I knew the family so they sent me to inform you, we will be taking a statement later but you can go the Royal Hospital now."

"Thank you, Arthur, oh sorry Constable Makin," Gladys replied she felt better now at least her husband was alive.

Jimmy went with Arthur to the front door and he put on his helmet, he asked Jimmy if he knew why anyone would attack his dad.

"I suppose they wanted to rob him can't think of any other reason."

As Arthur walked away Jimmy thought nosy suspicious sod.

Jimmy and Gladys entered the long-tiled ward with a fireplace at the end, they found him sitting up in bed with his left leg up on a track and his left arm in a sling and a bandage around his head, he looked pale and had a black eye. Gladys bent over and kissed Albert and started crying she sat down by his bed and took his right hand in hers.

"Don't worry love it looks worse than it is I'm a tough bugger I'll recover."

Jimmy went over and kissed his dad on the cheek they were a very demonstrative family and had no issues showing their feelings for each other. Albert recalled what he could remember from the previous night, leaving the Atlantic on the dock road leaving at 10:30 and walked towards the pier head to catch a bus home. Someone had come from behind and hit him on the head and dragged him towards the docks another person had joined him and there they both beat him and threw him to the floor and had lost conciseness. Jimmy had an idea who it could have been. Albert asked his wife if she would go and ask the nurse for a glass of water, when she had gone Albert turned to Jimmy.

"I'm sure it might have been the Smith brothers I've heard they are out of jail and they may be out for revenge for helping to get their dad put away, I knew we shouldn't have returned to Liverpool."

Six years ago Albert had upset their father Tommy Smith Snr by mistakenly moving in on their territory selling stolen goods from the docks, Tommy had got his two sons to attack Albert and he had retaliated by setting up Tommy and getting him arrested, Albert had been scared of repercussions so had got his family out of Liverpool and moved to London, but Gladys couldn't settle so before moving back Albert had asked his Liverpool contacts about the Smith family and was informed they were all in jail, so had returned home, now he was afraid they had been released and were out for revenge. He couldn't say anymore as his wife retuned. The sister asked them to leave and return later because Mr Cartwright needed to rest. As he drove his mum home Jimmy promised himself, he would find who had attacked his dad but had a feeling who it was, and it wasn't the Smith brothers.

Later Jimmy waited outside of Paton Calvert's in Binns Road where Chrissy worked, he watched the men and women spilling out of the gates and saw Chrissy talking to a couple of women, he drove up and sounded his horn she turned and was both surprised and pleased to see him, she climbed into the car leaned over and kissed him. "I wasn't expecting to see you yet although I'm pleased, what's the matter you look upset?"

"I'm unable to take you to Uncle Jack's tonight Chrissy my dad is in hospital he was beaten up last night and robbed."

"Oh, Jimmy how awful who would do such a bad thing to your dad is he hurt very bad?"

Jimmy told her about his dad's injuries Chrissy was upset she liked Albert. "Please give your dad my love when you see him, I can't believe it was Arthur to tell you was he nice to your mum?"

"He was," Jimmy told her but omitted to tell her about Arthur's questioning of why his dad would be attacked.

When Chrissy got home, Arthur was at her parents' with Norm they all looked at her.

"Has Arthur told you about Jimmy's dad?"

"Yes," her brother replied.

Madge looked shocked. "What a terrible thing to happen his wife must be in a right state."

Chrissy's dad asked what he was doing in a pub like that it's got a bad name.

"I don't know, Dad. He works on the docks maybe he knew the men who drink there."

"It shouldn't make any difference where he works Norman a man should be able to drink wherever he wants without the fear of being attacked," Madge replied.

Chrissy asked Arthur if the police had spoken to Albert. "Yes, they spoke to him this afternoon but he told them he didn't see their faces and he had no idea why he would be attacked he thinks it might have been just to rob him but he only had ten pounds on him, we think the motive might be more than just robbery judging by his injuries."

"Should you be discussing this Arthur I don't like the way you are making more of this."

Arthur's face turned red, "Just amongst us Chrissy of course you will find out more from Jimmy."

"If I do, I will not be discussing their private life with you it's their business and nobody else's." Chrissy then went up to her bedroom to get away from Arthur's suspicious thoughts.

It was two weeks since the attack on Albert, Jimmy had asked around all the pubs on the Dock road and Scotland road asking if anyone knew where the Smith brothers hung out as yet he had come up with nothing, he began to wonder if he was wasting his time looking for the brothers but he had to rule them out before he could find the real culprits. He had not seen Nosey Jones or Roachy he dare not go the Grove Inn where Goff and his minders hung out but Jimmy had a suspicion the attack on his dad had a lot to do with Goff. His dad was still in hospital but was recovering well from his injuries although it would take time for his broken leg and arm to mend. He saw Chrissy at the weekends, but they had not been out since the attack. To make it up to her he asked where she would like to go this coming Saturday, it was his mum who had suggested they go out, she had told him, your only young once Chrissy is a lovely girl and told him to look after her, Chrissy had suggested the cavern although it wasn't his kind of music, he had told her they would go there. He would spend the rest of the week searching for the whereabouts of the Smith brothers.

Chrissy was in May's house and told her about them going to the Cavern.

"We're going to the Cavern this Saturday I don't think Jimmy is too fussy, but he agreed to go I've never been to the Cavern and now the Beatles have left."

"Do you think he would mind if me and Gary went, we haven't been out on a foursome for ages or do you want to be alone with him, you've been going the hospital to visit his dad."

"I don't mind May I'm sure Jimmy won't mind it will be a laugh."

When May returned home her brother Norm was there with Jean, she told him about Saturday and that May and Gary were going too, Jean asked if they could go as well. "I thought we were going the pictures," Norm replied.

"We can go there anytime Norm it's ages since I've been to the cavern."

Chrissy phoned Jimmy from the phone box in Everton Road the next day and told him about the others wanting to go with them, he hesitated he didn't want Jean there she might slip up and give the game away. "Bloody hell Chrissy, I thought you wanted us to be alone?"

"Well, we won't be alone at the Cavern, will we?"

"You know what I mean—ok then sorry I sounded a bit narked then I have things on my mind, I will meet you at yours then get the bus into town and meet the others there, I'm leaving the car at home see you Saturday."

There was a click as Jimmy hung up Chrissy felt a bit upset, he usually phoned her back and spoke longer, maybe he was still worried about his dad.

# Chapter 11

## The Cavern 24<sup>th</sup> August 1963

Jimmy was standing in the dank cellar of the Cavern club watching Chrissy, May, Gary Jean and Norm dancing to the Swinging Blue Jeans, he had a smile as he watched Chrissy; she was laughing and thoroughly enjoying herself he had had a few dances and was now sipping an orange juice, he hadn't noticed Jean leaving the dancefloor he only had eyes for Chrissy till he heard her voice behind him. "Are you alright, Jimmy? Haven't seen you for a while have you fell out with me."

"Haven't you heard? My dad is in hospital I have been busy visiting you're the last person I want to see now, so please keep your voice down in case anyone hears you."

Jean was a bit upset with his attitude towards her so asked him how his dad was, Jimmy told her he was due home on the 3rd of September he was slowly recovering. "I'm going to Blackpool for the August bank holiday with me mam, Chrissy and her mum, dad and brother; we arranged it before my dad's attack so he can't go now."

"Norm didn't mention going to Blackpool to me."

"We did ask Norm, but he told us he was saving for your wedding in case you're wondering."

Chrissy and the others joined them, and Jimmy turned away from Jean who was looking angry. Jean was not happy how dare Norm make that decision without asking her she would have loved to join them in Blackpool. Jimmy then went with Chrissy to dance to Good Golly Miss Molly, Norm asked Jean to dance but she declined.

"Why did you refuse to go to Blackpool with the others you should have asked me first it would have been fun."

"I thought we were supposed to be saving love if we want to get married in May I don't want to move in with our parents I want a place of our own I thought you wanted that as well."

Norm was easy going he would do anything for Jean but, lately she had turned moody and wanted to be taken to fancy clubs and restaurants which he could not afford, Norm thought she could be a bit jealous of Chrissy because Jimmy took her to those places and now, they were going away for the weekend with the family. He did wonder sometimes how Jimmy could afford those treats and own a car Norm often felt that Jean would prefer Jimmy than him.

After they left the Cavern, each couple went their separate ways Jimmy took Chrissy's hand as they walked towards the bus stop. "Jimmy, I'm so looking forward to our trip to Blackpool, I'm glad your dad persuaded your mam to go she told me she felt guilty going while your dad was in hospital."

"He told her it was silly to miss out just because he couldn't go and told her they would have plenty of chances of going away together."

"Your parents are so devoted to each other I know mine are, but they don't often show their feelings in public."

"I know they have taught me to be the same as right now I'm going to kiss you now." He laughed and kissed her in front of people standing in the bus queue.

The bus arrived and they managed to get on but had to stand, they reached the end of Everton Road and walked slowly towards Northumberland Avenue with Jimmy's arm around her waist.

"I don't think Jean is happy with our Norm refusing to go away with us she seems a bit moody lately and I don't think it's just the Blackpool trip, I just hope she is not changing her mind about marrying him."

Jimmy hoped not as well he didn't reply immediately because he too was worried about the change, she was becoming too clingy. "If she does change her mind, he will be having a lucky escape," he replied with feeling.

Chrissy was surprised about his attitude towards Jean and looked at him in surprise. "Don't you like Jean?"

"I don't particularly care one way or the other about her."

They walked on in silence Chrissy wondered why his mood had changed so suddenly when he seemed to be enjoying himself, she didn't realise that Jimmy didn't like Jean.

"Are you OK Jimmy? You don't seem as happy."

He smiled, "Of course my love just got things on my mind."

He took her to a quiet place out of sight and took her in his arms and kissed her hard on the lips, he then whispered in her ear. "I love you Chrissy take no notice if I'm a bit quiet sometimes…look why don't we ask your mum and dad if we can get married sooner maybe next June I will pay."

"Thanks Jimmy but they would feel insulted if you offered to pay, I am their only daughter I know they could afford to give me a good traditional wedding, maybe we could discuss it with them I'm sure they wouldn't object to you paying for the cars or something, but yes I will ask I don't want to wait much longer either."

After kissing more Jimmy took Chrissy to her front door and told her he would flag down a taxi.

"I will see you next Friday at the train station goodnight Chrissy."

That same night Norm was taking Jean home, she was quiet, and he was worried he had noticed some change in her lately.

"Are you still cross with me because I refused to go to Blackpool or are you changing your mind about marrying me?"

Jean stopped walking and turned to look at him, he looked better with a moustache, it made him look more mature he had his hair cut into the style of the Beatles and he looked like Ringo Starr the Beatles drummer, she had changed his clothes style as well he was wearing a polo neck sweater, grey slacks and a black leather jacket he now looked trendier.

"I'm not so much mad at you just a little disappointed because you decided for me without asking my opinion, I know we are saving but can't we just live with me mam for a while till we have saved more, we are only young once we need to live a little."

"I would prefer a place of our own love where we can both relax if we move in with your mam you might feel settled and be reluctant to move, no, I think it's best to find our own place once we have settled, we will have plenty of time to enjoy ourselves before the children come along."

They had reached her home in Bootle and Jean noticed the lights were off. "Do you want to come in for a drink before you go home Norm?"

He was tempted he knew what she wanted she had no shame in showing him, was he normal he asked himself any other man would jump at the opportunity, but he still wanted to wait because that's how he had been bought up to wait till you were married show respect. He had a suspicion that she was no virgin, but he loved her. He took her in his arms and kissed her softly on the lips he felt a yearning in his groin he was a man after all but ignored it.

"No thanks love I will get home now I will see you on Friday."

Jean opened the door feeling frustrated what was the matter with him? Did he have no passion in him he was certainly different from Jimmy who was very passionate, oh how she missed his lovemaking maybe he would return to her bed again, she knew he loved Chrissy but could not for the life of her understand why?

Jimmy had returned home and poured himself a whisky, he put the gas fire on and sat in the armchair his dad always used. He had wanted to buy a sofa bed and put it in the front parlour for his dad, because of his broken leg and arm he would not be able to manage the stairs, at first his dad had refused stating he would manage after a lot of cajoling and his mam promising to share the sofa bed he had relented. He was looking forward to the trip to Blackpool although he would be sharing it with others as well as Chrissy. He hoped they would get a chance to be alone. He was glad Norm had refused Jimmy did not want to spend much time in Jeans company she was getting a bit moody and everyone was noticing the change in her but despite that he liked spending time in her bed she was a very experienced passionate woman. He loved Chrissy with all his heart, but she was still determined to wait till they were married before she let him make love to her. He finished his drink and turned off the fire and went to bed with two women on his mind.

### Thursday 5th September 1963

Chrissy was in her bedroom playing *At last* by Etta James, she was lying on the bed with her eyes closed listening to the lyrics and thinking of Jimmy, most of the time they were together he was loving and funny making her feel as if she were the only girl who existed he was very attentive and still tried to make love although she was very tempted, sometimes though he would be moody, hardly speaking he was like he was in some kind of world of his own where she was not wanted, but, she loved him to distraction he was in her thoughts 24 hours a day seven days a week. While they were away in Blackpool her parents had took Gerry to the fair and were then taking him for something to eat later Jimmy's mam had been invited along Jimmy and Chrissy had refused telling them they were going to Stanley Park then Blackpool Zoo. They had returned to the hotel to change and their parents were still out they went to Jimmy's room that he shared with Gerry, he had started kissing her then pushed her onto the bed and had started to undress her when they heard their parents return, luckily the room she shared with his mam was in the next room so Chrissy had picked up her jumper bag and shoes and had dashed next door before they had got to the third floor they were on. Just how far she would have let him go she had no idea but knew it was close. After that near miss it seemed as if her parents had guessed what had happened and there were no more opportunities to be alone again, but they all had a good time in Blackpool. She had been to see his dad since he had been released from hospital on the Tuesday and she had seen him yesterday. They had set up a bedroom in the front parlour with a new sofa bed Jimmy said it would come in handy if anyone wanted to stay. They had then gone out to meet Tony he was with a young girl nearer Chrissy's age and seemed to be better than his usual girlfriends. Her name was Susan and Chrissy and she had a lot in common and talked about the latest record from the Beatles and the latest fashions. Jimmy had gone with Tony to the men's toilets most likely to talk Chrissy thought.

"Where did you and Tony meet?"

"I'm Billy's sister you know Billy, don't you?"

"Not really I have only met Tony."

"Billy and Ritchie are Jimmy and Tony's mates I was out with me mates and we saw them in the pub me and Tony got talking then he asked me out, I have been seeing him for six weeks now and I'm moving in with him next week."

"Must be serious then I never thought Tony would ever settle down what do your parents think about you moving in with him?"

"Oh, me, Dad isn't bothered it gets me out of his way, me mum died three years ago and since then it's just been me and Billy, we look out for each other our dad is never home."

"I am sorry to hear about your mum Susan every girl needs her mum mine is a bit old fashioned but I love her and couldn't do without her."

"Chrissy, can I tell you a secret you won't tell Jimmy will you in case he tells Tony, I don't want to tell Tony yet till, I'm sure."

"Are you sure you want to tell me you don't know me we have only just met."

"Chrissy, I need to tell someone if you don't want to know I understand."

Chrissy could see the girl was worried and could see tears starting to form.

"I think I might be pregnant I don't know what to do."

Chrissy was shocked; Tony had most probably forced himself on her. Jimmy and Tony returned so their conversation stopped. Chrissy looked at Susan then told them she needed to go the ladies Susan understood and followed her, once inside Chrissy told her to visit the doctor to make sure she was pregnant then tell Tony, it was then up-to him to decide if he would marry her. After they left the pub, she asked Jimmy how old Susan was, she was both saddened and shocked to hear that Susan was only seventeen.

# Chapter 12

Friday 6th September 1963

Jimmy had discovered where the Smith brothers hung out and was on his way to see them, he had Billy and Ritchie with him just in case there was trouble. He was informed they hung around a snooker club in Granby a tough area of Toxteth, they found the club which was based in the cellar of a three storied terraced house. They walked down the stone steps which were greasy and littered with used cigarette butts, The windows had iron bars and over the black iron door the sign Granby club was hanging loose, the door opened onto a room which was badly lit the air was filled with thick smoke you could not make out the faces of the men standing at the bar in the far corner, the talking stopped as they entered and the silence was scary as if you had lost your hearing not even a sound of glasses clinking, men of all shapes and sizes and different nationalities stared at them. At the back of the bar, they could see steps leading to what they presumed the snooker tables, Jimmy asked the barman for three pints of bitter and the talking resumed, Jimmy asked the barman if the Smith brothers were here the barman just nodded his head and pointed towards the other room, Jimmy asked his friends to remain in the bar but to keep their eyes on the pool room. He walked down three steps into the room which housed four snooker tables the only light came from a bare bulb hanging over the tables. Jimmy didn't know what the Smith brothers looked like so walked over to one of the tables where two men were playing, he watched while one potted the blue ball. "Are you the Smith brothers?"

While he waited for an answer, he took in their appearance, one looked to be in his thirties he was of medium build slightly balding and had a thin long face, the other brother looked younger he had a larger frame lots of dark wavy hair and had dark eyes that were not unkind.

"Who is asking?" The younger one asked. "I'm Jimmy Cartwright. You may have heard of my dad, Albert."

They looked him up and down and liked the arrogance of the young man the younger brother smiled showing white even teeth. "Yes, we have heard of Albert, he had our dad and us put away why do you ask?"

"Did your dad ask you to beat my dad up four weeks ago?"

They both laughed everyone stopped to look it wasn't very often they heard the Smith brothers laugh.

"He would find it difficult telling us to do anything young Jimmy he is dead, died two years ago from the pox don't give a shit about the dirty bastard, but he passed it on to our lovely dear mam and she died in agony she suffered we hope he did too, so, no, we didn't beat your dad up all that it's all water under the bridge now we have no argument with your dad."

Jimmy gave a sigh of relief and asked them if they wanted a drink. While they had a game of snooker with the brothers Billy and Ritchie had joined them they had told Jimmy they knew who it was that had beaten his dad, the brothers told Jimmy they knew everything that went on and knew he had worked for Goff who they hated, they told Jimmy what he had already guessed that Goff had got Nosey Jones and Roachy to take revenge on Jimmy by beating his dad. Jimmy swore he would get revenge and the brothers told him they would help in any way they could because they wanted to get rid of Goff and take over his money lending scheme. Jimmy told them he would deal with Jones and Roachy and they could deal with Goff.

Chrissy and May were out that same night at their local pub Gregson's Well.

"It's good to get out Chrissy it's not very often we get a chance to get out ourselves since we have met our fellas, but we are still best friends."

"When is your Arthur getting engaged? He has been going out with Rose since February when they met at the Grafton."

"I think he is stringing her along Chrissy, I really like her she is so nice and friendly, Mum thinks the world of her and would love her in our family, but I think he still has hopes for you."

"Well, sorry, he will wait forever I'm marrying Jimmy, I asked Mum and Dad if we could get married next June, Dad was reluctant asking why we couldn't wait longer but Mum said she doesn't mind she thinks Dad does not want to let go of his only daughter, but he eventually gave in when I told him I would always remain his daughter, have you and Gary decided on a date yet?"

"We are thinking of July 1965, because mam is on her own it will take longer to save; Gary's parents are helping with some of the expense they will pay towards the reception they are booking one of the hotels in Liverpool."

"Gosh, that is posh hope you don't turn snobby."

"As if, I'm working class and proud of my roots, but his parents are not snobby they are really down to earth, by the time I get married you will probably be having a baby or will have one."

"I hope so May a boy first just like Jimmy then a girl just the two what about you?"

"I don't mind what I have but two is enough for me as well."

Tony's girlfriend Susan had gone to the doctors who had confirmed she was pregnant, his attitude towards her was with contempt shaking his head and with a scowl on his fat face he told her that at her age she should not be having sex and that he could not condone her having a termination, it's against the law he had told her and that she would have to live with her mistake, he had asked about the father and had asked her if she knew who the father was. She had replied she knew who the father was and that she was not a prossy and didn't sleep around. She left the unkind doctor and headed for Tony's flat wondering how he would take the news. He had been shocked but wasn't angry.

"I should have been more careful love but I don't think either of us are ready to be parents yet, kids are a big responsibility you're only 17, do you really want to be stuck at home not going out having a good time, we will have kids later when you're a bit older and when we are both ready."

Susan told him about the nasty doctor and what he has said, Tony pulled her onto his knee.

"Horrible bastard don't worry I will sort something there is hardly anything there yet not a proper baby so it should be easy enough I promise you everything will turn out right so come on get dressed up and I'll take you out for something to eat and drink."

The next day Tony had found a woman who carried out abortions in the back room of her house in Tuebrook he arranged a day and time for Susan to see her.

## Monday 9th September 1963

Tony took Susan to the address in Tuebrook, they stood outside a big rambling Victorian terrace which had large sash windows on the first and second floors then a small window in the roof, the front garden was well cared for and had a bush by the side of the gate. The front door had paint peeling and the net curtains were thick and hid the interior. Susan felt very nervous she didn't really want to do this in her mind it was murder, but Tony insisted it was not a proper baby he had told her he would look after her when it was over and to stay off work and stay in bed, she would be fine. Tony rang the bell and after waiting a short time the door was opened by a woman who looked to be in her sixties, she was small and well-rounded she had white hair swept up into a rather untidy bun, she wore a long black skirt a grey blouse and a wraparound pinny which was clean. Susan glanced at her hands which were also clean and her nails.

"Hello, my dear you must be Susan, Tony you go for a drink for a couple of hours come on Susan lets hurry you follow me."

Tony felt relieved he needed a drink and was glad he didn't need to stay, what a bloody pickle he thought I didn't need this to happen, Susan is a nice girl but that was the problem she was only a girl. He had made sure she had not told her brother Billy otherwise he would have been beaten to a pulp by now. He sat down with his drink while he waited to collect her. She had been taken down a long hallway to a backroom, the room was small it had a sink a bed that was covered with a plastic sheet and a table that had what looked like a long pair of pliers Susan shuddered.

"Well, then, dear take off your drawers lie on your back with your knees up and apart."

Susan woke she felt groggy she didn't know how long she had been out for; she felt a terrible pain in her belly and her insides felt sore.

"Your awake at last, you fainted here take these aspirin and put your drawers back on and put this pad in, the bleeding will stop once you have had a good rest take more Aspirin to stop the ache it will hurt for a while, but it will feel better…"

The bell rang. "Here is your fella at last, he is late." She went to the door and told Tony to wait in the hall, when Susan emerged Tony was shocked Susan was deathly white her eyes looked huge and there were dark circles underneath, she could hardly stand, and she was shaking.

"Bloody hell Mrs what have you done to her?"

"She will be fine in a couple of days get her home into bed and place a plastic sheet beneath her, keep her warm with plenty of fluids and aspirin I promise she will recover."

Tony thought she was trying to convince herself as well as him, he drove her home in the van put her to bed and gave her some soup and more aspirin.

"I will kip on the couch tonight my love I'm sorry you have had to suffer like this, hopefully you should feel better tomorrow try and get some sleep."

The next morning Tony went into the bedroom to wake her he got no response, he noticed that her face looked translucent and she felt stone cold, he pulled back the covers and recoiled in horror as he saw a pool of thick brown blood and the smell was awful, she had bled to death the stupid old bitch had killed her. Tony stood there crying he had never cried before what was he going to do? If he called the ambulance the hospital would know she had had an illegal abortion. He stood there for what seemed like hours but was only minutes as his mind thought of what he would say to the doctors.

Later, after her body had been removed, he had told the police who had been informed by the hospital that he had been out and returned to find Susan fast asleep in bed so he had sat up and fell asleep on the settee then found her when he had gone to wake her, he had not known she was pregnant and she must have arranged to have the abortion. He was genuinely upset and told the police he would have married her if had known she was pregnant. The police told him how sorry they were and tapped him on the shoulder and left. He had to face Billy next and decided he would tell him the same story as he told the police.

## 17<sup>th</sup> September Anfield Cemetery

A small crowd gathered around the grave of Susan McAllister, the wind was light, and the temperature was cool, the sky was overcast with the sun hardly casting its warmth and light over the mourners. Although Chrissy had only met her the once, she couldn't forget the young girl who had seemed so meek and mild, she must not have told Tony she was pregnant and was scared so had an abortion instead she felt angry at Tony. Jimmy stood to her left and Tony to her right he did look genuinely upset, on the opposite side of the open grave stood Billy her brother whom she had only just met he was different in looks to his sister he was stocky taller than Jimmy and had a mop of fiery red hair like his father who stood by him he was also stocky but not as tall as his son he didn't seem all that upset over losing his daughter and Chrissy thought what a hard man he seemed. Chrissy was shocked when she heard what had happened and she blamed Tony, she told Jimmy what Susan had told her that time they had met and she told Jimmy she blamed Tony, they had a small disagreement because Jimmy always defended Tony he told her it takes two to make a baby, but she had replied saying he should have used protection it shouldn't be left to the woman all the time. Jimmy had replied telling her it was a problem they would never have which had hurt her feelings. But he had called around to her house with a bunch of red roses apologising for upsetting her. Now as she heard the priest say ashes to ashes dust to dust, she took a handful of soil and threw it in the grave which now held Susan's coffin.

# Chapter 13

20<sup>th</sup> September, 1963

Albert had the plaster removed and after a short while he returned to work. Jimmy had told him who was responsible for the attack on him and told him he would get revenge.

"The Smith brothers have set up a meeting with Nosey Jones he thinks he is going in on some deal with them he won't know it's me he is meeting."

"Do you want me to go with you?"

Tony handed Jimmy a knife, "just in case you need it."

"I won't I will use my fists."

After a lot of persuading from his dad Jimmy took the knife. They were in the Stanley Albert had just finished work and had met his son and Tony for a quick pint.

"Is it true Tony you have another girl so soon after Susan's demise? You didn't waste much time, did you?"

"Yea I liked Susan a lot, but Cissy approached me she told me she had fancied me for ages I couldn't upset her by turning her down, could I? Anyway I have learnt my lesson she has started on the birth control pill so there won't be any more mistakes."

Jimmy and Albert looked at each other and started laughing. "What are you laughing at?"

"You're not daft, are you? You selfish get making her take precautions while you enjoy yourself," Albert replied.

Tony shrugged. "I hate those French letters." His face looking pained, they all started laughing.

"Are you seeing Chrissy tonight son?"

"Yea we're going the pictures later she wants to see Dr No with Sean Connery she thinks he is gorgeous she loves his sexy voice."

"Oh, so you have a rival," Tony laughed. Jimmy smiled and told him no he was her number one love of her life.

Albert finished his drink and told them he had better get going. "I'm taking your mam out tonight for a meal then down to the County for a sing-along are you coming Jimmy?"

"I'll be seeing you after the pictures I'll have another drink with Tony."

After Albert left Jimmy told Tony he was going to meet Jones on the sunday night at the Salisbury dock when he sees me, he will get the shock of his life.

Chrissy was getting ready for the pictures they didn't usually go the pictures Jimmy wasn't all that fussy on sitting watching pictures he preferred going to clubs to dance and listen to music, she had persuaded him to go and watch Dr No she wasn't sure if she would understand the film because Jimmy had told her it was about spies but she did rather like Sean Connery he was handsome and had a very sexy voice, of course it was only a fancy because Jimmy was her love and he too was handsome. Chrissy looked in the mirror scrutinising her features, her nose was straight and not too big her eyes were large and a warm brown, her lips were full and as Jimmy kept telling her very kissable. Her dark brown hair was shiny and very thick which hung to her shoulders. She hardly wore much make-up because he told her she didn't need much her complexion was perfect, so she wore a little amount of eye shadow in a light brown and pink lipstick. Chrissy decided to be casual so decided on a skinny rib polo neck jumper in a soft pink and a dark blue mini skirt. After checking once more in her mirror she went downstairs to wait for Jimmy. Her dad Norm and Gerry were talking about football they were going to Goodison to see Everton play Sheffield Wednesday and Gerry who had been to his first match earlier in the year and saw Everton draw had been disappointed not to see any goals so was looking forward to watching another game. Chrissy's mum was in the back room watching All our yesterdays.

"Hi, Mum, are you getting away from all the football talk?"

"Hello, love you look very smart what time is Jimmy calling for you?"

"Not for another fifteen minutes do you want me to leave you to watch your programme in peace?"

"No, where are you going tonight?"

"We are going the pictures for a change to watch a spy movie."

Chrissy didn't like the film she didn't understand what was happening, Jimmy told her he had enjoyed it despite him not wanting to go. They went to meet his parents in the county pub and join them for a drink and a good old sing-along.

"Hi Chrissy, Gladys greeted them, did you enjoy the film?"

Jimmy laughed, "it was Chrissy's idea to go but she didn't like it I liked it she only wanted to see Sean Connery."

"I don't blame her he is gorgeous, and I love his sexy voice."

Both Jimmy and Albert groaned and lifted their eyes. "Well come on you two go and get the drinks in," Gladys remonstrated.

That same night Norm and Jean were out at Gregson's Well which was a well-known venue for folk singers like the Spinners, it was still early so the pub was quiet. Jean was wearing a blue blouse with a plunging neckline, a black leather mini skirt and black leather boots, she was thinking about Jimmy he had returned to her bed sometimes they went to a boarding house if her mum was home or parked up and made out in the back of his car, she knew he only saw her for one reason but she didn't mind—or did she? She felt slightly guilty for two-timing Norm because he was a nice bloke, he did his best to keep her entertained, she had asked him to take driving lessons so they could have a car, but he had told her he couldn't think of that yet because he was not earning enough money.

"Penny for them love."

Jean looked at him her thoughts about Jimmy interrupted.

"Just thinking how time is passing so quickly only eight months till we get married."

"I can't wait I see there are a couple of houses for rent in the next road to ours I might enquire about them now what do you think love?"

"I'm sure if we wait till nearer the time, we might find somewhere else I fancy Bootle or maybe Walton."

Norm didn't respond immediately he was disappointed it was obvious she didn't want to live near his parents but why did she want to live in Walton?

"Well, what do you think?"

"OK if you want to live there, we will look next year but it's not very often houses come up for rent Walton is a popular area."

### Saturday 21st September

Chrissy and her mum were shopping in Great Homer Street, her dad and two brothers and Gerry's mate Georgie had gone to watch Everton v Sheffield

Wednesday at Goodison. Gerry had been so excited the previous night they had trouble getting him to go to sleep, after threats from his dad telling him he won't be going if he didn't settle down, he had finally gone to sleep, he had woken early that morning because he had dreamt, he had missed the game because they all slept in. Chrissy was due to see Jimmy later they were staying in at Jimmy's and listening to music in his front parlour. After Chrissy and her mum finished shopping, they sat down and had a welcome cup of tea and a cream cake. It was nice and quiet without the men and her brother Gerry.

"I had better start the tea they will be home soon, and no doubt will be hungry."

Later the house erupted with noise as her dad and brothers came into the kitchen singing, Gerry ran in shouting. "Mum, we won, we won yippee."

Her dad and Norm wore big grins like Cheshire cats. "What was the result then?" Chrissy asked laughing at their antics.

"We won 3-2 Dennis Stevens, Roy Vernon and Alex Young scored is that right dad?"

"Yes, Gerry that's right."

"OK, Gerry go and get washed, your tea is ready. Chrissy, will you lay the table for me? It seems like you all had a good time by the looks on your faces I don't know who the kid is you two or our Gerry," Madge laughed.

After tea and telling his mum and Chrissy about the game Gerry settled down and was reading his comics he yawned.

"I think it will be an early night for you Gerry," his dad told him.

Chrissy washed the dishes while Norm dried their parents were watching the telly. "Is everything OK between you and Jean she seems a bit quiet lately hope you don't mind me mentioning it."

Norm stopped drying and turned to his sister. "So, you have noticed has anyone else?"

"Yes, as a matter of fact, May and Arthur have noticed, and Mum asked me as well."

"I don't know sis I have asked if she is alright and if she had changed her mind about marrying me, but she was shocked and told me she loves me, she wants things I can't afford-now she wants me to learn how to drive so we can have a car. I think she sees you with Jimmy going out to those clubs and taking you out in his car, but I have explained over and over I don't earn as much as

Jimmy and we are saving to get married, she wants to move in with her mum but I want a place of our own."

Chrissy felt sorry for her brother he was a brilliant brother and a good decent man she felt anger towards Jean, but she couldn't tell him how she felt because it was obvious, he loved her.

"I'm very happy that Jimmy does take me to those places and he has a car but I would still be happy if he didn't it's him, I love not what he spends on me, Jean should realise that it's you that matters and not material things I know. I'm biased but she is lucky to have you as a future husband."

"I'm the lucky one sis and thanks for that vote of confidence I will have another talk to her later she is coming here tonight, can I borrow your record player and records? Especially the Tony Bennett and Frank Sinatra ones get her in a romantic mood."

"Of course, bruv those two would get anyone into a romantic mood."

Chrissy and Jimmy were in his parent's front parlour listening to a new LP Jimmy had got from his mate who was a steward on a liner going to New York, it was a black female singer called Nina Simone the song they were listening to was *No good man* her voice was rich and easy to listen to. Chrissy and Jimmy were sitting on the bed settee and Jimmy had his arm around her. He started sneezing and coughing. "Are you alright? You sound like you have a bad cold."

She felt his forehead it felt hot

"I think you should take a couple of aspirins you have a high temperature."

"I am feeling a bit rotten," he admitted he never usually let colds bother him, but this time was different.

Chrissy went through to the back room and asked his mum where she kept the aspirin, she told Gladys that Jimmy had a high temperature. Gladys gave him two tablets and two clean hankies.

"I think it would be best if I went home and let you have an early night."

"Do you mind love I feel awful about this—Mum will you ring a taxi for Chrissy."

"It's OK I will get a bus."

"No, you will get a taxi home no arguments." He took out a five-pound note and gave it to Chrissy.

When Chrissy arrived home her parents looked surprised. "Your home early everything ok?" her mum asked.

"Jimmy isn't well he has a bad cold and cough so has gone to bed, but he made me come home in a taxi."

"Good lad he is looking after you it's dark now he doesn't want you walking around by yourself," her dad replied.

Later as Chrissy got ready for bed, she hoped he would be OK he hadn't kissed her goodnight in case he passed on his cold she missed his kisses and hoped she would still be able to see him tomorrow.

## Sunday 22<sup>nd</sup> September, 1963

Albert and Gladys were concerned, Gladys had gone to wake Jimmy for breakfast but could not rouse him she had felt his forehead and it had felt very hot, after giving him aspirin and plenty of water he had fallen asleep but had woken with a rasping cough.

"Do you think we should call the doctor out Albert? It's that cough it sounds chesty to me."

"Let's see how he is love he hates fuss I'll take him some of that soup you made."

When Albert entered his son's room Jimmy was awake. "How are you feeling son? I have some homemade soup try and manage that."

Jimmy took the bowl but only managed a small amount. "Sorry I can't manage any more tell Mum its lovely I do feel a bit better it's just this cough that is bothering me."

"Your mum wants to call the doctor out what do you think? Do you want to see him?"

"No, Dad. I'll be OK I'll just stay in bed all day and see how I feel later will you phone Mrs Makin and ask to speak to Chrissy and tell her I won't be able to see her today but tell her not to worry."

"Ok, son have another sleep it will do you the world of good."

It was after 10 p.m. and the house was still. Jimmy climbed out of his warm bed and put on a thick woollen jumper, corduroy trousers his pea coat and boots, he opened his bedroom window which faced onto the back yard threw out a rope and tied one end to the leg of his heavy wardrobe, that should take my weight he thought although he still felt bad, he had to go out to meet Jones. He climbed out of the window and grabbed the thick knotted rope and climbed down he stood on the canopy over the kitchen and took a breather then lowered himself down onto the concrete floor of the back yard, opened the back gate ran up the entry into the road which was now deserted he climbed into his car and pulled away.

Jimmy parked the car down a side street on the Dock Road and walked towards Salisbury Dock which was situated on the north side of the dock system, the wind was becoming brisker as it swung a pub sign from side to side, he entered the dock using a torch to guide him, he could hear the River Mersey crashing against the dock wall, the dock was a small area made with different sized granite blocks and there was a tower located between the dock entrance, as Jimmy hid behind the tower to wait for Jones it had started to drizzle with icy rain which ran down his neck he shivered but felt very hot, the moon was now hidden behind a cloud which moved slowly across an overcast sky, he hid in the shadows his nose was dripping with the cold he had and with rain drops which had now turned into a heavy down-pour, he was beginning to think Jones wasn't going to show when he heard footsteps and a small light from a cigarette, he waited the light got nearer he spoke softly Jones? Nosey is that you he shone the torch towards Jones face, Jones blinked. "Who is it? Are you one of the Smith brothers?"

Jimmy stood out from the shadows and at that moment the cloud covering the moon scuttled across the leaden sky leaving Jimmy in its full light which reflected in the puddles. Nosey dropped his cigarette and stuttering asked. "C...c...c...artwriight, what are you doing here?"

Jimmy walked towards him scowling. "I've come to talk to you about the attack on my Dad, Jones."

"I...I...I don't know what you mean never touched your dad you have the wrong man Cartwright."

Jimmy was feeling weaker he had a coughing fit but recovered quickly and ran at Jones with all the strength he could muster and pushed Jones against the wall.

"Ahhh," Jones cried out at the pain in his back.

"You are a lying bastard, it was you and Roachy, was it Goff who told you to attack my dad?"

Jimmy had his arm up against Jones throat, Jones nodded his head Jimmy loosened his arm. "Why him why not me?"

"Goff told us to get your dad because he is older and weaker than you and he told us to finish him off, but we didn't did we? We thought it was going a bit far killing him, are you ok? You don't sound too good to me."

"I'm OK don't think you're getting away with the attack."

The rain was now lashing down harder with the wind blowing rain into their faces he noticed that Jones look scared he could feel himself weakening, with great effort he punched Jones in the stomach and his face Jones fought back then Jimmy used his torch to hit Jones over the head, Jones pushed him back and in his weakened state Jimmy felt himself falling back as he fell he grabbed Jones coat and they both fell to the wet dock floor and the torch rolled away-Jones was now on top of him with his hands around his throat Jimmy gasped for breath, he then remembered the knife, he pulled it from his coat pocket and plunged into Jones stomach, his hands fell from his throat and he stood and looked down at the knife protruding from his stomach which was oozing with blood, Jones pulled the knife out and dropped it to the floor. Jimmy heard the angry river smashing against the dock wall he stood and picked up the knife he noticed Jones running towards him he made one last effort and pushed Jones who fell backwards into the grey dirty river with a big splash there was another splash as the knife followed Jones into the River Mersey. Jimmy staggered away and passed the pub which was lit up and noisy no one left the pub so unseen Jimmy sloped away into the dark night and managed to drive home despite his head feeling heavy and his chest feeling like someone, or something was laying on him.

Albert had got up to get a drink and went into Jimmy's room to see how he was, he was shocked to see the window open and a rope hanging down into the yard below. Albert pulled the rope in and closed the window then hid the rope under Jimmy's bed it was now 11.30 and it was blowing a gale and raining heavily, where the hell is he thought Albert, he grabbed a pair of pyjamas from Jimmy's tall-boy and went downstairs to wait for him to return home, he turned on the gas fire in the front parlour poured himself a whisky and waited. It was just after midnight when he heard a car pull up outside without turning on the hall light, he opened the front door to catch his son before he headed for the yard, Jimmy climbed out of the car and was hunched over, his cough which now seemed worse was like a dog's bark that seemed extra loud in the eerie silence of the night. As Albert watched his son struggle, he stepped out and walked over to him. "Come on son let me get you inside your soaked to the skin."

Once inside without a word exchanged Albert stripped his son of his wet clothes and began to dry his shivering hot wet body, he felt like he did years ago helping his little son get ready for bath night, there was no embarrassment Jimmy was too ill and Albert too concerned. After drying Jimmy and putting on his warmed pyjamas and Alberts's dressing gown he sat him down by the fire and poured him a whisky. After drinking a couple of whisky's Jimmy seemed to become aware of his surroundings.

"Where the bloody hell have you been you have made yourself worse."

"I went to meet Jones, dad, between raging coughs he told his dad what had happened, he is dead I have killed him he is now in the dock."

Albert was speechless, after a long interlude of silence Albert asked,

"Why tonight your ill you should have waited like I told you to."

"I told you Dad, I needed to sort it tonight I might not have had another opportunity, but I only intended to hurt him I didn't intend to kill him it was me or him in the end."

"I still think you're a bloody fool, but you had to save yourself now get to bed before your mam wakes up, I've put a hot water bottle in your bed, I'll sort out your wet clothes and rope tomorrow."

It was 6 a.m. when Gladys woke, Albert was already up she wasn't to know he had stayed up with Jimmy sitting by his bed, she went into Jimmy's bedroom and noticed Albert he had fallen asleep, and his head rested on the bed. Jimmy was now delirious and was shouting out 'Jones' and something about the Mersey, he was sweating profusely but also shivering, Albert woke and saw his wife standing on the other side of the bed with her hand on her son's brow.

"Albert he is worse how long have you been up?"

Albert didn't answer he was now fully alert. "I'll phone the doctor now I think he has pneumonia."

It was now 7.00 and Dr Dove was upstairs examining Jimmy he turned to his parents and with a look of concern he confirmed that Jimmy had pneumonia. "Can I use your phone to call an ambulance?"

"Of, course doctor," Albert replied and led him to the phone in the hallway. Dr Dove replaced the receiver after requesting an ambulance as soon as possible. "The ambulance won't be long Mr Cartwright try not to worry he is a strong young man, and we have a good success rate of treating pneumonia with antibiotics."

Albert thanked the doctor and told him they should have called him out yesterday. When the ambulance arrived and they had carried Jimmy down on a stretcher and put him in the ambulance the doctor told the crew his diagnosis and told Albert and Gladys they were taking him to Fazakerley Hospital, Gladys asked if she could go in the ambulance with Jimmy and the doctor said yes. Albert told her he would follow later after phoning his brother to ask for a lift.

At the hospital Jimmy was made comfortable, they had placed an oxygen mask on him, and the ward doctor had just left him, the sister in charge told Gladys she could go to see him but not for long. Albert arrived just as Gladys was leaving the ward. "How come your leaving so early?"

"The sister in charge wouldn't let me stay any longer I told her you were on your way, and she told me they would let you see him but only a short while he is sleeping now."

Albert was led to Jimmy's bed he seemed a bit calmer now he had stopped calling out and was sleeping peacefully, after a short while he was asked to leave and to return at visiting time, he found his wife being comforted by Jack his brother she noticed Albert and ran into his arms, she looked up at him her face was blotchy and her eyes were red. "Oh, Albert we should have called the doctor yesterday."

"I know love, but he didn't seem so bad yesterday."

Albert thought if he hadn't gone out to meet Jones, he would have been alright, Jack gave them a lift home and told Albert he would take them the hospital later. Albert called the dock and told his boss what had happened he then phoned Jimmy's boss and told him Jimmy was in hospital. Gladys asked him about phoning Chrissy. "She will be in work now I will call around to the house later and tell her, but I will ask her to wait till tomorrow to visit."

Later that evening Madge opened the door to find Albert on the doorstep.

"Hello, Albert everything ok? How is Jimmy? Sorry, how rude of me; come on in."

"Is Chrissy home? I would rather wait and tell you all together if that's ok?"

"She is upstairs getting changed."

Madge called her daughter downstairs, Chrissy walked into the kitchen and saw Jimmy's dad standing by the table, her mum, dad and brothers were sitting down all looking at Albert.

"Hi, Mr Cartwright how is Jimmy?"

She noticed his ashen face he usually had a smile for her, but he was frowning Chrissy felt sick with dread had something bad happened to Jimmy. "I'm sorry Chrissy Jimmy is in hospital he has pneumonia he is quite bad at the moment but don't worry the doctors say he is a strong young man and has a good chance of recovery with antibiotics, he is on oxygen at the moment to help with his breathing I know you would like to see him immediately but can you wait till tomorrow evening the staff only allow two people to visit and we would like to see him this visiting time."

"Of, course it's only right his parents see him first."

Chrissy felt disappointed she couldn't see him tonight but understood that Albert and Gladys had more right to see him than she did. Albert told her that his brother would take her to the hospital tomorrow then left.

Chrissy sat at the table then began to cry. "What would she do without him."

Madge went to her daughter and put her arm around her shoulder. "There, there you heard what his dad said, the doctors think he has a good chance of recovery."

Her dad put a cup of tea in front of her. "Drink this I have put a small drop of brandy in you have had a nasty shock."

Chrissy was reluctant at first then sipped at her tea she wasn't fussy of the taste, but the warmth of the brandy soothed her. "I don't want nothing to eat, Mum. I want to lie down."

"It's no good starving yourself you will need your strength to cope with the upset."

Later, in her bedroom after eating a small amount of food Chrissy put on her music and played *The Good Life* and thought of Jimmy lying in hospital which led her to cry again, she didn't hear the words as her sobs drowned out the voice of Tony Bennett, Oh Jimmy please be OK please god look after Jimmy help him get better, Chrissy then fell asleep dressed on the top of her bed.

Arthur was on duty at Westminster Road police station when a call came in that a body had been found in Salisbury dock, it was being investigated by the detectives at Cheapside, all they knew at this time was that it had been spotted by a docker who was unloading a load from a ship, the body had floated to the surface his sergeant told him they would know more later when the corpse had been examined by a pathologist.

# Chapter 14

Later that evening Albert and Gladys went to the hospital to visit Jimmy, he was still asleep, but his breathing seemed easier they had removed the oxygen mask. Gladys sat by his bed and took his hand it felt warm she squeezed his hand but got no response, Albert noticed her tears beginning to form and whispered. "Don't worry love sleeping will help him recover?"

"I feel so helpless just sitting here watching him sleep."

"If he wakes hopefully, we will be here so come on smile so if he wakes, he will see your lovely smile."

After an hour visiting time was over, they both kissed Jimmy on his cheek and left. Albert phoned Chrissy and told her Jimmy was still sleeping and told her he would see her tomorrow.

Norm and Jean were sitting watching the television they hardly spoke because her mum and sister were sitting with them. Jean was bored she was thinking about Jimmy in hospital, selfishly she thought about herself missing out on going out in Jimmy's car and missing out on his lovemaking, she thought why are we sitting here with mum and her sister watching television like an old couple.

"Norm, shall we go for a drink? I'm fed up sitting here watching the telly."

Her mum and sister both looked at her in surprise. "If we are in the way Jean just let us know and we will sit somewhere else," Margaret told her with a hint of hurt in her tone.

"I'm sure Jean didn't mean to upset you Mrs Simmonds come on Jean lets go the Mereton."

They arrived at the Mereton in Mereton Road Bootle it was a Monday night therefore it was quiet after buying the drinks Norm sat down had a sip of his pint and asked Jean why she was, fed up. "I think you upset your mam Jean you kind of implied she was in the way you didn't even answer her when she spoke to you."

"I was bored Norm sitting watching telly with my mum and sister like an old married couple and discussing Coronation Street we're only young."

"When we get married some nights we will be staying in and that's one of the reasons why I want our own place so we can be alone, we won't be able to afford to go out every night."

The next day Tuesday Chrissy could hardly concentrate on her work, she was a machine operator making household goods if she didn't concentrate it could cause an accident. She was looking forward to visiting Jimmy in hospital and couldn't wait for five o'clock to arrive.

The same time that Chrissy was thinking of him Jimmy woke up and was sitting up in bed, the doctor had told him the antibiotics were working and he was slowly recovering but needed to stay in hospital a bit longer as he still had some fluid in his left lung. He was hungry the nurse gave him some lunch which had just arrived on the ward he ate it with relish and enjoyed the strong cup of tea as well.

That evening Albert and Gladys arrived to collect her with Alberts's brother, as she waited outside the ward, she felt nervous she felt that a band had been tightened around her stomach.

"Don't worry Chrissy I'm sure he will be OK you and Gladys go in first, then me and Jack will see him after."

The ward door was opened as the visitors piled in, she followed Gladys to Jimmy's bed which was by the nurse's desk in the middle of the ward, Jimmy was sitting up chatting to the young man in the next bed. Both Gladys and Chrissy said 'Oh, Jimmy' in delighted surprise.

"Hi Mum, Hi Chrissy."

Although he was still pale his smile lit up his face, Gladys and Chrissy kissed him and he told them what the doctor said. "Cheer up you can't get rid of me that easily I'm a fighter."

After 25 minutes of small talk Gladys told Chrissy to have five minutes alone with him before his dad and uncle took over from them. While they were alone Jimmy said with a twinkle in his eyes. "I wish you could join me in here."

Chrissy laughed.

"I can tell your getting better trust you to think of something like that, she took hold of his hand, I thought I was going to lose you and all the time I felt sad that I had not shown you how much I love you, I promise when you are better, I will prove to you how much."

Jimmy saw his dad and uncle walking towards his bed and took hold of Chrissy's hand. "I will make sure you will keep to that promise come and visit tomorrow."

Albert arrived with his brother and pecked Jimmy on his cheek. "Good to see you awake son your mam told me what the doctor said we can't wait to get you home."

When Chrissy arrived home her mum, dad and brothers were watching telly, they all looked at Chrissy waiting to hear news about Jimmy, she need not have uttered a word they could tell by her beaming smile and her glowing cheeks that he was on the mend. Chrissy went to see her friend May whom she had not seen for a while. Chrissy told May about Jimmy and asked what May had been doing since she last saw her.

"I have good news Gary has been promoted and because of his rise in salary we have decided to bring our wedding forward to next year 21$^{st}$ August in St Georges Church."

Chrissy jumped up and gave her friend a hug. "May, that's three weddings within four months."

"That's not all I have also been promoted to secretary for the account's manager it's only temporary for one year while his is on maternity leave, but my salary will be higher, and I will. Be able to help Mum with the expense, Gary's parents offered to pay for everything but Mum thanked them and told them it was up to her to pay but would welcome any help."

May had some bridal magazines to help her decide what dress she wanted. Chrissy had already picked her wedding dress and had decided that May was to be her chief bridesmaid and Jimmy's cousin's little girl. May told her she would be matron of honour and her two little cousins as bridesmaids.

## 30$^{th}$ September 1963

Jimmy was discharged from hospital and was told by the doctor he would need to recuperate for two weeks before he returned to work. Gladys told him to sleep on the bed settee in the front parlour where it was warmer. While his mum went shopping his dad who had taken a day off work sat down by Jimmy.

"I know I have asked you before but now your better I might get more sense out of you, why the hell did you go out that night I know you said it couldn't wait, but it could have ended up with you in the dock and not him didn't you think of the bloody consequences think how your mum might have reacted to your death it would have broken her heart."

"Well, it wasn't me although I didn't mean to kill him that's him gone next is Roach."

"Leave it now Jimmy it's over now they might not bother us again."

"I can't, Dad. While Roach and Goff are around, you and Mum and Chrissy won't be safe Goff will get his revenge and it won't be me it will be the ones I love to hurt me."

"I understand Jimmy but leave it for now till your fully recovered remember what the doctor said, take Tony or someone else with you, no, don't argue you need to be prepared next time, while you were in hospital Jones body was found the next day the police still don't know who it is but it's got to be Jones, no one has reported him missing yet."

"As far as I know dad, he had no family and Goff wouldn't give a damm and Roach is most probably terrified he might be next."

"Yea, your right but as soon as I am able, I will get Roach just beat him a bit and tell him to fuck off away from Liverpool."

Chrissy was helping her mum wash the dishes after their tea. "Are you going to see Jimmy tonight love."

"No, Mum it's his first night back home. Gladys wants to fuss him so I thought I would stay away so they can spend time together."

"That's very thoughtful of you."

"That's what Gladys said when I rang to tell her I won't be calling round; you and dad will have to go out with them one night you will enjoy yourselves Gladys and Albert are lovely and so easy to get along with."

"Yes, we will Chrissy when everything settles down and Jimmy is better, we will be delighted to go out with them."

The next night Chrissy was sitting next to Jimmy in the front parlour, the fire was on the main light off and there was a soft light from the table lamp giving the room a cosy feel. They were listening to Frank Sinatra singing *Witchcraft* Jimmy leaned over and whispered. "Do you remember your promise to me?"

Chrissy blushed, "I do Jimmy."

"I want to arrange somewhere nice I don't want our first time to be in the back of my car your better than that or somewhere seedy I want to make it special; I was thinking we could go away for a couple of nights."

"I'm not making excuses but that would be awkward explaining to my parents about staying away for a weekend they will guess it will be with you."

"You're not changing your mind, are you? If so, it doesn't matter I don't want to force you if your still not ready."

"Jimmy, I do want you to love me I'm just thinking what Mum and Dad will say."

"Ok, love leave it with me I will think of something but right now I want to kiss you."

He took her in his arms and slowly and gently kissed her then forced her lips apart with his tongue and explored her mouth which set her heart beating faster, his kisses then became more passionate. Chrissy responded by kissing him back just as passionate and pulled him towards her, he pushed her back and placed his hand inside her jumper and slowly caressed her breasts his breathing became harder and she could feel his member pushing against her leg as he lay on top, then she remembered where they were his parents were right next door, she pushed him away they were both breathless. "Jimmy, not here please your mum and dad are only next door they could have walked in on us."

"Sorry, got a bit carried away I have missed you Chrissy and I'm thinking by your eager response you have missed me as well."

"I have but let's wait till we are somewhere a bit more private."

When Chrissy went to say goodnight to Albert and Gladys, Gladys looked at her and frowned she was flushed and her hair was messy, it seemed like Gladys had guessed what they had been doing but didn't comment. When she got home, she was glad her parents were in bed if her mum had seen the state Chrissy was in, she would have certainly had something to say.

### Monday 14th October 1963

Jimmy had returned to work he was in his office of the insurance company he worked for checking his client's files. He hated this job it was boring, but he needed it as cover to hide his money lending scheme. He was good at his job all his clients liked him he was always friendly and always willing to help if the less well-off couldn't pay him, his wealthier clients also liked him especially the women, they would invite him in and offer him a drink and sometimes more, at first he had he had accepted what was on offer from the older women because they were less complicated, till one day he had nearly been caught by one of their husbands returning home early. Now he had Chrissy he wasn't bothered, and he had Jean to relieve him of his sexual desires. Jean, she was becoming a problem, she was too clingy, last night he had gone to her flat and stood outside hidden from view he had waited and saw her close the curtains he stood out and she had saw him and invited him in. She was alone. "Hi, Jimmy how are you now," she had asked he had told her he was much better and told her he wasn't staying and told her he wouldn't be seeing her again in this way. She had cried and told him they were suited for each other and that Chrissy was too goody, goody and Norm was a good bloke but boring, she told him he had enjoyed their time together and that Chrissy wouldn't be as good as her in bed, "You love making love to me," she had goaded, after her vitriol about Chrissy she had gone quiet she had known she had gone too far. He had lost his temper and told her it was not making love because she was a slag. "Don't make me laugh it's not making love it's just sex why would I give up a decent woman like Chrissy for a slag like you?"

He had realised he had gone too far when he saw her face fall to the floor and heard her gasp in shock at his cruel words. He felt terrible he had placed his arm around her shoulder and told her he was sorry for calling her a slag but told her she knew from the beginning of their affair what the outcome would be she was marrying Norm and him marrying Chrissy. Jean had stopped crying and looked at him with her big hazel eyes and told him she knew but couldn't help falling in love with him, she asked him to love her one more time he had taken her to her bedroom and made love to her for most of the night.

Later that evening after collecting money from the clients of the money lending scheme, Jimmy felt guilty about last night he shouldn't have given in to temptation how could he face Chrissy knowing he had cheated on her again, especially when she had promised she would let him make love to her. He had an idea for them to spend time together but wanted to ask Chrissy first he would have to forget about Jean and make sure he made a fuss of Chrissy. The next evening, he called around to Chrissy's she was both glad and surprised to see him as they had arranged to out that Friday and go to a club. They sat in the front parlour Jimmy making sure no one would hear them spoke softly and told her his idea. "I'll take you to Chester for the day because it's too cold for the sea-side, I'll book a room before we go, later you phone next door and tell your mum my car has broken down and we can't get home because we have missed the last train. I know it's only one night but it's better than nothing, what do you think?"

"What time would I ring? I don't want to wake Aunt Maud and Mum up if it's too late."

"Ring about 11.00 it will be a Saturday so surely they won't be in bed that early."

"Ok, I will have to hide an overnight bag in your car before we go when are you thinking of going?"

"Next Saturday will that be OK?"

"Yes, that's great for me."

"Brilliant Jimmy was pleased he grabbed hold of her and kissed her then pulled back, the rest can wait till next week."

He saw the look of worry on her face. "Don't worry love I will look after you I promise you it will be fine, and you will enjoy it."

Arthur was still seeing Rose, but he wasn't sure where the relationship was going, she was a nice enough girl quiet and shy but no fool, she didn't badger him about getting engaged which made him wonder if she really felt anything for him, he wasn't sure if he loved her because he still had feelings towards Chrissy. He had been to the station at Cheapside and asked if they knew the identity of the body found in the dock over three weeks ago, he was told they were no closer to finding out who it was. It had stayed inside the dock and had not drifted out to sea because it was rather stormy that Sunday night and the tide was in.

"How come no one has reported him missing?" he had asked and was told someone had looked at the body but told them it was not the person he was looking for.

That person had been Roach he hadn't seen Jones for a couple of weeks and had heard about the body being found so just to be curious he had gone to the police pretending to be looking for a friend who had gone missing, which of course some of it was true, he felt sick when he had seen Jones but showed no emotion when he lied to the police it was not the person he was looking for. He felt scared who had killed Jones? He knew he had a meeting with one of the Smith brothers for a deal was it one of the Smith brothers? Would he be next."

Arthur had heard about Jimmy going into hospital on the Monday so put the idea that it might have something to do with him out of his head, he still didn't trust him, since he had returned to Liverpool he had taken the chance of persuading Chrissy to go out with him out of reach Chrissy had fallen for Cartwright hook line and sinker, he blamed himself he had been too slow and rued the day Cartwright had turned up. Cartwright seemed to have a lot of spare cash how could he afford a car and take Chrissy to those fancy restaurants and

90

nightclubs. It wasn't just jealousy that Arthur felt it was a feeling that Jimmy was up to no good and it was up to him to keep a close eye on Cartwright to make sure Chrissy came to no harm.

# Chapter 15

Jimmy and Chrissy booked into the Swan Hotel in Chester, Chrissy had bought an overnight bag with a change of clothes for that evening because he was taking her to a good restaurant and then dancing, she had brought a new black lace negligee and a black cocktail dress, she wanted to look like a sophisticated young lady rather than the inexperienced teenager she was. As they unpacked in their bedroom which had a fancy four poster bed and heavy red velvet curtains surrounding it, she couldn't believe she was staying in this posh hotel, they even had their own private bathroom. Chrissy felt nervous she was looking forward to tonight but was also worried, Jimmy was sexually experienced she was a virgin, what if she failed to make him happy? Because to Jimmy sex was an important part of a relationship. She watched him unpack he had bought his suit on a hanger which was in a plastic cover he also bought his shoes in a shoe-bag, he was whistling he turned to see her watching him and winked, when he did that, her heart fluttered, he was so handsome and sexy.

"How do you fancy going the zoo? It's cold but dry what do you think?"

"I would love to Jimmy."

They caught a bus which took them straight to the zoo, they had a good time making faces at the monkeys and gorilla, exclaiming how they loved the wild cats and how smelly the elephants were, Chrissy didn't like the snakes but loved the little tiger cubs, they only shared a sandwich because they wanted to save their appetite till later.

Back at the hotel Jimmy suggested they have a drink in the bar till it was time for them to get changed for their night out, Chrissy had a gin and tonic while Jimmy had a whisky and soda, it was warm in the bar and busy there were older couples also in the bar looking very glamourous and suave they kept glancing over to where Jimmy and Chrissy sat and giving them curious looks, Jimmy whispered:

"Look at them looking down on us bloody old snobs."

"Jimmy! That's not very nice how do you know their looking down on us they might be wondering why we are here we seem to be the youngest couple."

She had to admit she was feeling uncomfortable under their scrutiny.

"Come on Chrissy let's take these drinks to our room then get changed before we go back into the bar the table isn't booked till 7.30, we have a couple of hours yet."

Back in their room Jimmy sat on the red leather settee and patted the seat. "Come on sit down and finish your drink, have you enjoyed yourself up till now."

"I have it was fun going the zoo I haven't been since I was a kid have you been the zoo before?"

"Oh, yes I went with all the family a couple of times when I was a kid it was great fun with all my cousins, we took a hamper the weather was hot and us kids ate and drank loads then on the way home on the bus we were all sick, ha, ha, great times."

"Family mean a lot to you Jimmy."

"Yes, they do I'll do anything for them especially Mum and now I have you I'll do anything for you, when we marry you could give up work or you could carry on till we have kids which I hope wouldn't be too long, I'm an only child so I would like four kids two boys two girls."

"Good heavens Jimmy, you have it all worked out it's me that will have the kids, I might not want that many if any at all."

Chrissy kept a straight face and saw disappointment cloud his face. "I thought you wanted kids?"

Chrissy then laughed, "Oh, Jimmy of course I want kids especially yours."

Jimmy picked up a cushion and threw it at Chrissy who then ran to the bed and threw the pillow at Jimmy, he ran over and pushed her on the bed and kissed her very hard and forceful, she responded and threw her arms around his neck and returned his passionate kisses, he lifted his head and looked at her his eyes were now almost black with desire—he began undressing her slowly and deliberately looking at her while he did she unbuttoned his shirt and took it off then unbuckled his belt on his trousers he then pushed them off hastily, he was now naked the first time she had seen a naked man she glanced at his erect manhood and felt a bit shy and frightened. He kissed her again from her top to her bottom she forgot her shyness as she responded to his caresses, he teased her till she was gasping for him to take her, at first it had hurt but he was gentle and kept whispering he loved her she told him how much she loved him he took his time till she was satisfied then at the same time they climaxed. Chrissy lay in his arms she was now his she had proven how much she loved him she just hoped she had pleased him. After a couple of minutes Jimmy leaned up on his elbow and looking at her told her. "That was beautiful you are beautiful it was different with you because I love you, he looked at his watch and smiled, we have one hour to get ready so go now before I change my mind and keep you here all night."

Later at the Plane Tree Restaurant they had a three-course meal which started with prawn salad, rump steak dauphinoise potatoes with mixed vegetables then followed by a lemon meringue, they drank champagne which Chrissy enjoyed. Chrissy then phoned her aunt Maud next door and asked if she could speak to her mum after five minutes her mum spoke. "Chrissy, are you ok? Has something happened, where is Jimmy?"

"Sorry Mum, but we were on our way home and Jimmy's car stopped he can't get it going there are no garages open and we have missed the last train, we will have to find a cheap bed and breakfast and stay the night separate rooms of course."

There was a long pause, "Mum? Are you still there?"

"Yes, Christine I just hope this is genuine and you have both not planned this, why leave so late? You should have left earlier; I think your dad will have something to say to Jimmy when he sees him just behave yourself."

The phone went dead her mum had hung up on her. They went on to a dance hall called the Royalty Theatre and danced and drank till one in the morning they then returned to the hotel and Chrissy told Jimmy about her conversation with her mum. "I don't think she believes me I'm not looking forward to tomorrow she will just have to look at my face and guess."

"We will worry about that tomorrow she can't kill you or stop you from seeing me its 1963 so stop worrying and enjoy the rest of the night."

They didn't have much sleep they spent most of the time making love discovering each other's bodies and what they liked. While Jimmy slept Chrissy lay awake in his arms thinking of what she was going to say to her mum for the first time she had lied to her mum and she didn't like the feeling, it was dawn before Chrissy fell into a restless sleep.

Jimmy woke Chrissy it was light she hadn't slept much. "Come on sleepy head time for breakfast then make our way home, it was good last night did you enjoy yourself."

"I did thank you Jimmy but I'm not looking forward to seeing mum."

After breakfast they headed home, and Jimmy asked if she wanted him to face her parents with her.

"Thanks Jimmy but I will talk to Mum alone for now it might be better I don't want Dad shouting at you."

"Ok, love I will wait till you think it best to call round."

When Chrissy entered the house her dad, Norm and Gerry were out. "Hi Mum, its quiet in here today where everyone?"

Madge was preparing vegetables for Sunday dinner she stopped peeling and looked at her daughter. "They are out watching Gerry playing football, well, my girl what happened and don't tell me his car broke down is it working now? I wasn't born yesterday don't insult me by telling me lies."

"Is Dad angry with me?"

"He is disappointed in you and especially Jimmy, has he left you to face the music?"

"No Mum, I told him to go home, OK we planned to stay over we love each other we are engaged, I thought he was going to die I kept thinking I'm going to lose him and not know what it was like to love him properly it's not as if I do this all the time." She started to cry. "I'm sorry I lied, Mum but I'm not sorry I stayed with Jimmy, I'm going upstairs to change then I'll give you a hand with the dinner."

When their dinner was over and Chrissy went to help with the washing up her mum told her to go into the back room and play draughts with her brother. "I want a word with your dad he can help with washing the dishes."

Chrissy had noticed her dad seemed annoyed with her he kept looking at her with sadness in his eyes.

"I have had a word with Chrissy, Norman. She is a good girl OK she stayed out with Jimmy, but they are young engaged and in love, Jimmy is a good lad you said yourself you like him he won't just leave her to face the consequences if she is left with child, he loves her."

"Why couldn't they wait till they were married it's only eight months."

"Remember a young couple 23 years ago they didn't wait, and they are still happily married."

"Madge, which was different we didn't know if I would return home from the war, and I very nearly didn't."

"Our Chrissy thought she was going to lose Jimmy and suppose she thought it could happen again, how do you know our Norm isn't having a close relationship with Jean? Suppose you think that's alright because he is a man, look love I know you want to protect her you don't like the idea of another man loving her, but it doesn't mean she won't still be your daughter, she loves and admires you she will always be a daddy's girl married or not so make up with her and trust them not to make a mistake."

Norman thought of his wife's words she was right they were a young couple in love and his daughter was a lovely decent girl, unlike Jean, he doubted that his son wouldn't be the first man to have slept with her.

Jimmy arrived home as he entered the house, he could smell roast lamb, he walked into the kitchen where his mum was preparing vegetables. "Hi, Mum, something smells nice I'm hungry."

He went and kissed her cheek then yawned. "Where is Dad?"

"Gone for a couple of pints why don't you join him dinner won't be ready for another couple of hours yet but don't drink too much."

"Ok, Mum I think I will I'll just take my clothes upstairs and hang them up."

"Who did you go to Chester with Jimmy? Tony called in asking for you."

Jimmy looked away his face turning red. "It was Chrissy, wasn't it? I have told you to look after and respect that girl."

"Yes, Mum don't say anything I didn't force her she wanted to spend the night with me, we are engaged to be married it's not a sin."

"Maybe not to you and Chrissy but what will her parents think of you sleeping with daughter before you are married, I'm not criticising you or Chrissy you're old enough to know what you are doing it's her parents they seem old fashioned and believe their daughter should be walking down the aisle as a virgin, I just hope they don't her too much grief."

Jimmy went to the County pub and saw his dad and Tony; Albert saw Jimmy enter and walked to the bar to buy him a drink.

"Where did you go yesterday mate."

"I went to Chester with Chrissy."

Albert heard him and frowned, Tony smirked and asked. "You stayed overnight was it the same room?"

"Mind your own bloody business, Tony," Albert replied.

96

Tony told Jimmy and Albert that Roachy was back drinking in the Grove and the Stanley-on-Stanley Road. "He usually ends up in the Stanley and leaves about 10.30 he then goes to a house down Jersey Street I think a prossy lives there, it's usually quiet on a Tuesday night if we get him there and pull him down an entry we shouldn't be disturbed."

"Well done Tony have you been following him," Jimmy asked. "I had some help from Billy and Ritchie your dad wants me to go with you this time which is OK with me."

"Right Tuesday it is then give him a bit of a beating and warn him to leave Liverpool or he will get what Jones did."

"Is Cissy still living with you Tony?"

"Yea Albert, but she is getting on me nerves now keeps on asking when I will marry her, I told her. Look, love, what's the rush? You're happy living with me, it's better than being squashed in bed with your two sisters and going to the outside loo, I asked her to wait to see how things go."

Albert and Jimmy said their goodbyes to Tony and left him drinking, as they walked home Albert asked his son about Chrissy. "You can tell me to mind my own business, but Chrissy is a well bought up girl and I hope you looked after her, you know what I mean."

"As I have already told Mum she wanted to spend the night with me we are engaged, so let's just leave it there I don't want to fall out with you."

## Tuesday 29th October 1963

Jimmy and Tony were standing around the corner from the Stanley pub it was dry but had a chill in the air, it was 10:20 p.m. and they were waiting for the limping figure of Roachy to leave the pub. "I hope he is in there," whispered Tony, "Ritchie said he visits there regularly and brings a couple of bottles back for his prossy."

"Look, Tony there he is."

Roach appeared and started walking down the road, they looked around there was no one around and so followed at a safe distance, when Roach got to the road, he was visiting they jumped him and dragged him to an unlit back entry. "Hey, what the fuck are you doing?"

The bottles of beer had broken and were emptying the contents down Roach's trousers making puddles on the entry floor. "Paying you back Roach."

"Who is it?"

"It's me, Jimmy Cartwright surely you haven't forgotten me I'm hurt Roachy."

"What do you mean paying me back? You don't owe me anything."

"I do owe you for beating my dad up with Jones."

Roach gasped. "It was you who done Jones in we were told to by Goff we didn't have any choice you don't argue with him, he wanted your dad finished off, but we didn't."

"Yea that's what Jones told me but that's no excuse Roach you're getting what's owing to you."

Unbelievingly Roach started to cry. "Jimmy please I'm sorry if you're going to give me a beating then yea OK but don't finish me off like Jones."

Jimmy punched him in the stomach and the face then pushed his head against the wall, Roach slithered to the floor where Jimmy gave him a kick. "I'm going to let you go I didn't mean to kill Jones but, I'm warning you to leave Liverpool and don't come back, don't go to Goff otherwise you will end up like Jones."

Jimmy turned and Tony was just behind him, Roach stood up and ran at Jimmy with a knife in his hand, Tony shouted, "Jimmy look out then shot Roach in the back."

"Bloody hell Tony why did you shoot him."

"Look at him Jimmy."

He looked at the prone body of Roach lying on the entry floor and saw the gleaming silver of the knife in Roach's hand. "I didn't hear a shot how come?"

"I have a silencer I know your dad told me to get rid of it, but I thought it might come in handy one day, sorry Jimmy."

He looked at Tony, "You soft get you have just saved my life don't be sorry."

He grabbed hold of Tony and gave him a hug.

"What are we going to do with him Jimmy?"

He thought for a moment, "We will hide him for now don't think anyone will be coming down here tonight, later we will get the van wrap him up weight him down then throw him in the river he shouldn't float to the surface."

"His prossy will think he has done a bunk," Tony replied.

"I will get Ritchie to give us an alibi just in case I will pick you up later and get this sorted, then you can finally get rid of that gun."

After disposing of Roach, Jimmy went to bed it was 12:30 a.m. but by 2 a.m. Jimmy still wasn't asleep he couldn't stop thinking of what they had done, well, he thought this was going to be the last time he would be disposing of dead bodies, he had given all the information he knew about Goff to the Smith brothers it was up to them how they would deal with Goff he wasn't bothered. Finally, he drifted off to sleep thinking about Chrissy and the night they had spent together.

The next evening Jimmy, Tony and Albert were in Tony's flat sharing out the money from their money lending scheme. They had told Albert what had happened the previous night.

"I thought I told you to dump that gun on the heist we did."

"It's a good job I kept it otherwise Jimmy would have copped it, but it's been disposed of now."

"Good, no more bloody killings, where is Cissy?"

"She has gone to her bloody sisters to babysit again I told her to stay because I'm on the booze with you lot, so, Jimmy you got Chrissy to stay the night with you at last, what was she like? Was it worth the wait?"

"Shut up Tony I'm not discussing Chrissy with you making it seem sordid when it's not."

"Oh, come on mate you haven't been so shy before telling me about your sexual conquests."

Tony had a leer on his face, Jimmy jumped up and pulled Tony's head back by his hair and with his face close to Tony's he shouted at Tony to shut up and stop talking about Chrissy in a crude way.

Albert pulled his son away from Tony. "OK, son, calm down. I'm sure Tony didn't mean any harm, it's just the way he is."

He gave Tony a hard stare and shook his head. "Sorry." Tony ran his fingers through his dark wavy hair pushing it back into place. "I didn't mean any harm I don't want to fall out with yer Jimmy your me best mate."

"Come on you two let's get this money sorted then we go on a bender, make up you two."

Jimmy took Tony's hand and shook it, laughed then ruffled Tony's hair.

Jean was worried she had so far only missed one period it was two weeks late which was unusual for her, but lately she had been feeling nauseas not actually being sick but feeling ill just by smelling coffee, maybe her mind was playing tricks she was worrying about her forthcoming marriage and whether she would be happy with Norm, he was good and kind but was that enough? She craved excitement in her life she enjoyed going out and she enjoyed sex especially with Jimmy, oh how she missed him, his handsome features, his smile and the twinkle in his dark brown eyes but most of all his lovemaking. She thought back to the last time she had seen him the hurtful words he had thrown at her, then she smiled the making up in bed and the French letter coming off and the look of horror on his face. Jean knew there was no future for them he loved Chrissy, but if it turned out she was pregnant the situation would change, she smiled again she now hoped she was pregnant and Jimmy would have to marry her, she decided not to worry any more.

The same evening Chrissy was with her friend May playing Beatles records in Chrissy's bedroom. "So, you spent the night with Jimmy in Chester."

May had a look of wonder on her face.

"It was lovely, May. We went to stay in a posh hotel with a four-poster bed, then we went the zoo made love then went out to some posh restaurant then dancing then made love most of the night, I was a bit nervous and shy at first but he took his time and was very gentle with me, I'm so glad I did now."

Chrissy told her friend this with a dreamy faraway look in her eyes remembering the time.

"Oh, Chrissy what if you end up with a baby before you get married?"

"I won't. He used a French letter; I'm still getting married in church in white. Mum guessed what had happened and was cross with me at first but later seemed to understand and hasn't mentioned it since, Dad was a bit off with me but he seems OK just a bit awkward, Jimmy is calling around on Friday to babysit our Gerry with me while Mum and Dad go out with Albert and Gladys, I hope Dad will be OK with Jimmy."

"What was it like? You know making love did it hurt much?"

"At first, but not for long I think if you really love someone its good, Jimmy told me it was beautiful and better for him because he loves me."

"Me and Gary do a lot of petting but up to now he hasn't demanded more, if he asked me I would because I love him but I wouldn't suggest it because I think that's too forward for a girl, I wonder if your Norm and Jean have made love. It wouldn't surprise me if she suggested it. Oh, sorry Chrissy she is your future sister-in-law, I shouldn't be saying mean things about her."

"Don't worry I think the same about her she isn't good enough for our Norm she seemed nice at first, loud, but nice but now he seems so miserable you wouldn't think they are getting married in six months."

They put on another record on Gerry and the Pacemakers, *how do you do it,* then looked through some bridal magazines.

# Chapter 16

**Friday 1ˢᵗ November 1963**

Jimmy was nervous as he knocked on the door of the Bennetts, he hadn't seen Chrissy's parents since he had taken her to Chester, he wasn't sure of the reception he would receive especially her dad. Norm opened the door. "Hi, Jimmy come in mate."

They went into the kitchen where Chrissy Gerry and Jean were sitting at the table playing snakes and ladders there was no sign of her parents were, they avoiding him?

"Hi Chrissy, Gerry," bloody hell he thought, "What was she doing here? Hi, Jean."

Chrissy looked up she didn't look very happy. Norman then told Jimmy his mum and dad had left to go and meet his parents and had asked him and Jean to babysit Gerry, Gerry had told his brother he was not a baby. "I thought we were looking after Gerry?"

He looked at Chrissy who just shrugged. "They thought you would rather go out we don't mind do we Jean?"

Jean just nodded her head it seemed to Jimmy that she did mind.

"I've won!" exclaimed Chrissy. "I will just get my coat then we can go for a drink somewhere."

"Why don't all of us stay in get some drinks then have a game of cards it will be fun," Jean suggested.

"No thank you," Chrissy and Jimmy replied at the same time.

They went to the Gregson's Well and when Jimmy had brought their drinks Jimmy asked, "What was all that about you told them we would look after Gerry."

"They don't trust us being alone together that's what's it all about, they think we will be making out in the front parlour while Gerry is upstairs in bed, they are treating me like some kid, how do they know our Norm and Jean won't be making out but, of course it's different for our Norm he is a man."

Jimmy shrugged. "Don't worry it's just the way they are not worth getting upset about, anyway I would have put a chair in front of the door to warn us."

Chrissy looked at him he had a smile on his face and a twinkle in his eyes she forgot her bad humour and laughed.

### Friday 8th November 1963

Chrissy called around to Jimmy's who was alone. "Where are your mum and dad have, they gone out for the night?"

He smiled, "they have gone away to Llandudno for a dancing weekend with Uncle Jack and Aunty June we have the house to ourselves."

They had some drinks and danced to the music of Frank Sinatra, Tony Bennett and Etta James, they were dancing and smooching to *at last* when he took her hand and led her upstairs to his bedroom where they made love.

"It seems a long time since we have been together like this."

Jimmy whispered as they lay replete and entwined under the bedclothes. "It seems your parents are determined to keep us from being alone at ours, but they can't stop us making love anywhere else."

"I have been thinking Chrissy I think it's time I got a place of our own now we are getting married next year, if we buy something cheap we could get it decorated to our taste then when we do get married it would be all ready for you, you could choose the furniture and curtains then I could stay there till you are ready to move in, where would you like to live?"

"Can we afford to buy our house? What about here in Walton?"

"I was thinking Walton Hall Avenue they are nice big houses with a garden front and back I noticed one for sale as I drove past, would you like to live there with me and our kids?"

"I would love to Jimmy." Chrissy was excited she had seen those houses and had always liked them but never thought she would ever live in one.

"I will phone the estate agents tomorrow ask the price if it's not too expensive I will arrange a viewing don't worry I'll sort it I have the money for a deposit."

### Monday 18th November 1963

Jean had been sick again she now knew for sure she was having a baby, two monthlies missed and being sick proved it, as yet she hadn't been the doctors and she hadn't told her mum she hoped her mum hadn't heard her being sick, she had to see Jimmy urgently, she would call in to Norm's later to see if he was there and try and arrange a meeting with him. Norm had told her he and Chrissy were buying a house and felt jealous, Chrissy was full of it they had viewed it fallen in love with it and had arranged a mortgage, and Norm wanted to rent a two-up two-down in Everton, Chrissy was so lucky. Jean was disappointed to find Jimmy was not with Chrissy when she arrived at Norm's house. "Are you seeing Jimmy tonight, Chrissy?"

"No, he is busy tonight working overtime to pay for the house, once we get the contracts signed and exchanged, we want to start redecorating some of the rooms, some need modernising."

Bloody hell thought Jean I wish she would stop bragging I'm fed up of hearing it. "Come on Jean let's go into the parlour and listen to some music it's a lovely surprise you are turning up tonight."

Jean smiled but it did not reach her eyes, Norm noticed Jean was very quiet and she looked pale, even when he kissed her, she did not seem as eager as she normally was, he pulled back and looked at her. "You're looking very pale you're not even wearing make-up are you alright?"

"I think I'm getting a cold I thought I would be alright coming out tonight, I'm sorry Norm I will have to go home."

"I'll just get my coat and take you home."

"No, it's alright I will jump a black cab I'm not in the mood for waiting for a bus tonight."

Norm took a pound from his pocket and gave it to her. "You wait inside I will get a taxi and ask it to come here."

Later after he had seen Jean into the taxi Chrissy asked if Jean was OK. "She is starting with a cold she doesn't feel too good, and I must admit she does look pale I told her to have an early night."

When Jean arrived home, she told her mum she was going straight to bed because she wasn't feeling well. "Do you want a cup of hot chocolate, or Ovaltine I'll bring it in to you, I've noticed you haven't been looking too well recently."

"No thanks, Mum. I'll have a little read then go to sleep I need to be well for work tomorrow."

"See how you are tomorrow love if your no better stay off and rest."

"OK Mum, goodnight."

Margaret Simmonds went to the kitchen to make some tea for herself and her other daughter Jenny, she wore a frown she had heard Jean being sick but hadn't asked her if she was pregnant, Margaret was waiting for Jean to confide in her, she assumed it was Norm's, ahhh well they would have to bring their wedding forward. Jean meanwhile had got out her writing pad pen and envelopes from her bedside table and proceeded to write to Jimmy.

*Dearest Jimmy*

*I need to see you urgently I'm sorry I have had to write to your address but there was no other way of contacting you. Please meet me outside of North Park at eight o'clock next Tuesday, if you don't arrive, I will call at your house.*

*Love*
*Jean xxx*

The next evening Jimmy called at Chrissy's he had received two letters one from the solicitors in the morning and one whose handwriting he had not recognised in the afternoon when he had gone home for his lunch. He had opened the solicitors letter informing him the contracts were ready to be signed and exchanged, he had then opened the other letter and was shocked to find it was from Jean, his spirits had plunged he had felt a tight knot in his stomach and his hand shook. He guessed what was so urgent, she must be pregnant otherwise why would she write to him?

That afternoon at work he found it hard to concentrate, he was pleased about signing the contracts, then she had to come sneaking back into his life when he thought he had rid of her. He had always been careful always used protection, then he remembered that last time he had spent with her when the French letter had come off, bloody hell surely that one mishap couldn't have caught her, could it. He would just have to meet her next week and know for certain whether she was pregnant then sort something out. Chrissy opened the door and greeted him with a kiss. "Are you ok? You looked a bit worried then?"

"Yea I'm fine just work stuff I have some good news."

He took the letter from his pocket and handed it to Chrissy, she smiled. "Oh, Jimmy it's happening our own house I'm so excited."

He hugged her they were still in the hallway, "You need to ask if you can leave work early tomorrow, I will meet you at 3.30 outside of work we have the appointment at 4.30 at the solicitors."

Madge walked into the hallway. "Hello Jimmy, Chrissy why are you keeping him in the hallway come into the kitchen where he can sit and have a cup of tea."

Chrissy's dad looked up from reading the Liverpool Echo.

"Hello, Jimmy." Then went back to reading the sports page, he was still cool towards Jimmy he had still not forgiven him for spending the night with Chrissy if only they knew they were managing to make love while his parents were out, they must have guessed what they were doing but they trusted them and had a more modern outlook on sex.

Chrissy told her family they were signing the contracts tomorrow, her dad put down his paper and said, "You're both taking a lot on with a mortgage at your age those houses don't come cheap, do they?"

"It's OK Mr Bennett I have put a big deposit down my mum and dad had an endowment for me and claimed it when I was 21, I have kept it in the savings and have earned interest so the mortgage won't be that high, the house wasn't that expensive it needs a lot of modernising and that was reflected in the asking price."

"Dad, you need to trust Jimmy he knows what he is doing he deals with money every day so just be glad for us."

"We are glad for you aren't we Father?" Madge gave her husband a hard look that bode no argument. Her dad stood and took Jimmy's hand and shook it then hugged his daughter. "I'm sorry love take no notice to a fussy dad like me, I hope you will both be happy in your new home, are you moving in soon Jimmy? Chrissy will have to wait till she is married."

"Can we go into the parlour and talk dad?"

"Yes, but please leave the door open."

## Tuesday 26th November 1963

Jean stood outside North Park it was mild for the time of year, all day the sky was heavy with cloud now it had started to rain it was only a light shower, but she put up her umbrella she didn't want her hair to get wet, she was wearing a beige mackintosh, a pair of knee length black patent leather boots, a pair of capri pants and a red polo neck sweater. Jimmy pulled up and opened the window.

"Quick jump in before anyone sees us."

Jimmy drove to Burbank in Crosby and parked up. "Is it what I think it is your pregnant?"

"Yes, it must have happened the last time I think I maybe about two months I'm being sick in the mornings, how did you know I was pregnant?"

"Why else would you want to see me so urgently, have you been to the doctor to have it confirmed yet?"

"No not yet I know I'm pregnant."

"Is it mine? How do I know? It could be anybody's, I know what you're like."

"Of course, it's yours what do you think I am? I haven't been with anyone since you, you can't half be cruel sometimes Jimmy."

"OK shut up I believe you but, it's not going to change things I'm still marrying Chrissy—can't you persuade Norm to make love and blame it on him you can tell him it's premature."

"No, Jimmy that won't work what are you going to do?"

"You will have to get rid that's the only solution I will sort it and pay for the termination then we can get on with our lives you're not spoiling my chance of happiness with Chrissy I have plans for us."

"How can you be so casual about aborting your own child?"

"It's not even a real baby yet you need to do something now before it's too late—like I said it's the only way leave it with me and I will get it sorted, don't write to my address again I will get someone to put a note through your door when I've arranged something."

"This wouldn't have happened if Chrissy would have given in to your advances earlier, I heard she spent the night with you hope you enjoyed it."

He took her back to North Park and almost shoved her out of the car in annoyance then sped off.

Jean uttered bastard, you cold bastard you could have taken me nearer home because it was now raining heavily, and the wind blew her umbrella inside out.

When she arrived home her hair was stuck to her head like rats' tails, she felt miserable, her mum and sister were watching the telly. "I'm just going to get changed, Mum. I'm soaked to the skin."

"Ok, love I'll make you a nice hot drink would you like some jam sponge with it ."

"Just the cup of tea please, Mum," she shouted from her bedroom she didn't want her mum to see the tears which were falling down her rain-soaked cheeks.

Later in bed she made up her mind whatever he planned she would not be getting rid of her baby.

The next evening Jimmy called at Tony's flat he needed to talk to him. "Alright Jimmy? You just caught me in I'm just going with Cissy to her mam's."

He noticed the strain on his best mate's face which was unusual because he was normally a happy go lucky bloke. "Come in have a drink."

"Are you sure Tony? I don't want to spoil your night."

"Hang on a minute while I have a word with Cissy there is something bothering you and I want to help."

Tony went into the bedroom where Cissy was brushing her hair. "Do you mind if I don't come with you? Looks like Jimmy has a problem."

He went and sat on the bed and kissed her.

"I'll make it up to you on Friday take you somewhere nice for a meal."

She looked disappointed but told him she would go to her mums alone. When Cissy left Jimmy told him about Jean. "Bloody hell mate what are you going to do?"

"Can you contact that woman who does abortions?"

"You don't mean that one who killed Susan? Surely you don't want to risk Jean's life sending her there?"

"I can't think of anyone else mate."

He could see that Tony was shocked he maybe crude and sometimes selfish, but he did care. "Susan was small and delicate she was barely a woman, Jean is older and is stronger she will be able to cope with the abortion better, come on Tony help me I can't bear the thought of losing Chrissy."

Tony thought for a moment it was unusual for Jimmy to sound so desperate he usually took problems in his stride he had changed since he had met Chrissy. "Ok, I will go to the house and see if she still does abortions and get a date for you, when will be the best time?"

"Try for a Thursday then she will only need one day off work to recover she will have the weekend as well…"

# Chapter 17

**Thursday 28<sup>th</sup> November 1963**

Tony went to the address in Tuebrook, he felt very wary after what had happened to Susan Jimmy was taking a chance sending Jean to this place it was obvious the woman wasn't capable to carry out safe abortions. He fancied Jean and couldn't believe Norm hadn't taken her to bed, was he a man or a mouse? Given the opportunity he wouldn't have minded a chance with her she was good looking and had a body to admire and she seemed full of fun, he liked Chrissy, but she was too sweetly nice for him, and he knew she didn't particularly like him. He rang the bell and waited there was no answer then he lifted the heavy knocker and gave a few knocks after a short while he noticed the light come on in the fanlight above the door, which was then slightly opened he heard a chain put across the door, it was not 8 p.m. and he felt cold and wanted to get home as soon as possible. "Yes, who is it? What do you want?"

Tony saw a pair of blue eyes framed by gold rimmed glasses staring at him. "Mrs C, I was wondering if you still did favours for women in trouble?"

She opened the door wider. "Come in quick before anyone sees you." She led him into the long hallway, she gave him a long look.

"Have I seen you here before? Have you got the poor girl pregnant again why don't you marry her?"

"Yes, it was me and no she is not pregnant it's for a friend of mine."

He omitted to tell her what had happened to Susan, this was no time for recriminations. "Oh, yes that's what they all say."

"As I have told you it's my mate's girlfriend do you want to do it or not?"

"Ok, but I want five pounds up front then another five before I carry it out, is Monday OK for your friend?"

"Bloody hell Mrs that's a bit much it wasn't that last time; it will have to be a Thursday."

"I can't do next Thursday it will have to be in two weeks' time then I will be going away to look after my daughter so that's my final offer."

"OK Mrs two weeks' time then." He wasn't interested in what she was doing he just wanted to get out. "Tell your friend to bring her at seven o'clock I need an early night."

She held out her grubby hand, Tony counted the money into them he hoped they would be cleaner than they looked now. "Oh, by the way tell him to bring her around the back I will leave the back gate open I don't want the neighbours getting suspicious."

Tony called in to Jimmy's where he was taken into the back room. "All sorted take her to this address at seven, he handed Jimmy a piece of paper, go around the back the gate will be open I'll put a note through Jean's door tomorrow where do you want to meet her?"

"I'll meet her in the next road to hers at 6:30."

"OK, I'll go home now its bloody cold out there."

"Thanks Tony I won't forget this here, take this bottle of whisky have a drink to warm you up."

Jimmy and Chrissy had received the keys to the house and on the Friday went to see what needed doing, after having a good look they decided to completely knock out the old-fashioned kitchen and replace it with modern fitted cupboards and units with room for a fridge and a washing machine, the other rooms just needed brightening up with paint of light pastels. Chrissy was delighted and could not wait to go shopping for furniture and fittings, Jimmy decided to bring in builders for the kitchen and painters and decorators for the other rooms, Chrissy asked him if they could afford to pay for professionals and couldn't they paint and decorate themselves with help from their families.

"No, it will be quicker don't worry I can afford it just you concentrate on picking the furniture."

## Wednesday 11th December 1963

Norm and Jean were sitting in the front room of her flat, her mum was out at bingo and her sister was at her friends, they were watching Coronation Street, but Jean wasn't really taking much notice she was thinking about the next night.

"How are you getting on with your wedding dress fitting love?"

Jean came out of her daydreaming and at first wasn't sure what to answer. "It's coming on a treat Norm, looks lovely."

That was a lie she had put on weight, and she had a slight bump so had not been near the dressmakers for over a month. Norm hadn't noticed because he had not seen her without clothes and she now knew he never would, Jean hated this deceit, and she was sad there would be no wedding to this kind lovely man.

Norm was also wondering why Jean had changed so much from a lively outgoing passionate woman to this moody cold person she had become. He pulled her towards him and kissed her hard on the lips she was taken by surprise at his ardour and responded to his kisses, it was as his hands began to move over her body she drew away.

"I want you Jean I've been a fool don't let's wait I want to make love to you right now."

Bloody hell she thought he would have to wait till now, well it's too fucking late you dozy bastard she felt like yelling at him, but she just smiled. "Sorry love I'm not really in the mood I just feel so tired."

"I think you should see a doctor you seem to be tired a lot lately." he looked worried.

"I will Norm please don't worry."

As Norm was putting on his coat to leave, she asked him if she could meet him tomorrow, he was surprised they didn't usually see each other on a Thursday. "Of course, love where do you want to go?"

"Could you meet me in West Derby Road by the entrance to Newsham Park at eight, I'm going to a friend who lives in one of houses in the park it's a flat, I know we don't usually see each other on a Thursday but I need to speak to you about something important."

"Why not now? I'm in no hurry is everything OK."

"No, Norm I will wait till tomorrow I need to get to bed now goodnight love."

As Norm made his way home, he felt worried he had a feeling Jean was going to tell him their wedding was off or that she really was ill, otherwise her mum would have said something, maybe she was seeing someone else and that's who she was going to see tomorrow.

### Thursday 12<sup>th</sup> December 1963

Jean had just finished getting ready her stomach was in knots and she felt sick with nerves, tonight she was taking a chance it would mean losing Norm and Jimmy, but it was a chance she had to take she was not going to get rid of her baby she didn't care what Jimmy thought. Margaret Simmonds entered her daughter's bedroom hoping she would confide in her now.

"Are you going out, love? You don't look too well."

"Yes Mum. I'm meeting Norm."

"Why don't you ring him and ask him to come here I will give you some privacy."

"No, it's OK, Mum. I'm alright I could do with a walk and some fresh air."

"Ok, love make sure you wrap up well and enjoy yourself." Margaret pecked her daughter on her cheek and left her to get ready.

Jimmy was also feeling apprehensive, he was taking a chance taking Jean to this woman but what other choice did he have. He wasn't going to let her ruin his life with Chrissy, the house was almost ready to move into they had fun choosing the new colours for the walls and the colour of the carpets and curtains and the new modern furniture, Jimmy wanted a black leather settee, and he got his way after a bit of arguing, they made up later by making love on the carpet in their bedroom. He hoped that Jean would recover quickly from the abortion, and they could both get on with their lives and forget the whole sorry episode. As Jimmy left his he bade goodbye to his parents and told them he was meeting Tony who had told him to tell anyone he was at his flat.

As Jimmy drove Jean to Tuebrook he took a quick glance at her, she had only said a quick hi when she had climbed into his car but had not uttered a word since. She wore her usual amount of make-up the usual mini skirt and knee length boots, he noticed her hands placed on her lap they were slightly shaking, he placed his hand on her knee and squeezed it and she brushed it away. "Alright Jean? Try not to worry too much."

"Alright? What do you think Jimmy? It's not you that's going through this how do you expect me to feel?"

"It will be over in no time just rest when you get home and tell your mum you're just having a bad period she will look after you."

Jean didn't reply.

They arrived at the house where they entered the back way as instructed, he noticed a light on in what looked like the kitchen and knocked on the door, it was opened immediately by a woman who looked to be in her sixties. "Hello dears, young lady just sit there now young man I will take the other five pounds and you can return in a couple of hours."

Jimmy took five one-pound notes from his wallet and placed them in her hands which at least looked clean as was the kitchen, but it was obvious she was not going to carry out the procedure here. He looked at Jean who looked pale even with her make-up on and gave her a reassuring smile, but she just scowled at him and turned her head away. He walked back to his car which he had parked two streets away and climbed in, he just sat and waited instead of driving away because he wasn't sure where he could go and was it worth it. After about ten minutes or maybe more he heard a rap on his window he looked and was both shocked and surprised to see Jean looking into the passenger side window, he opened the car door and let her in then turned to her and asked what she was doing back so quick. "I'm not having the abortion Jimmy it's a life and I can't kill it."

"You can't have it you daft bitch how are you going to explain your pregnant to Norm."

"I'm going to tell him the truth tonight."

"Tonight?"

"Yes, Jimmy, I'm meeting him later by the park on West Derby Road so could you please take me there now."

Jimmy sped off without saying a word and headed for the Rocky Lane entrance to the park, Jean looked out of the window. "Where are you taking me?"

"I want a word with you so we will go this way in case Norm sees us."

"It's no use talking Jimmy I have made my mind up it's time Norm and Chrissy knew what you are really like."

They arrived in the park and Jimmy stopped the car there was no one around it was dark and misty and extremely cold, he turned to Jean. "So, you had no intention of having the abortion?"

"I told you didn't I don't want to get rid of my child."

"You, stupid mare I still won't marry you why spoil it for everyone?"

"I know Norm will still want to marry me and keep the baby that's how good he is but, it's you I love Jimmy and when I have your kid married or not, I want to give it your name and I want you to take responsibility to help me bring it up."

Jimmy was fuming and felt very worried he could see his future stuck with Jean and without Chrissy, he did not fancy it, he tried to reason with her, but she was stubborn, what was he going to do? He pulled Jean over to him as if to kiss her and she smiled and willingly moved over to his side, he took her by the shoulders then put his hands around her neck and squeezed, her smile froze and her eyes were wide open with shock she tried to fight him off but he was too strong, after what seemed a long time but was only a short time Jean's body relaxed and she was silent. Jimmy released her and her limp body fell sideways onto the passenger seat he looked at her body then came to his senses. "Jean, Jean, come on I'm sorry stop messing about."

He shook her there was no movement he looked at her, her eyes were open staring. "Bloody, bloody hell she is dead she is dead what the hell have I done."

He sat there thinking he looked at his watch it showed 8 p.m. she should have been meeting Norm, he drove further into the park his headlights shining eerily into the thickening mist. He got out and checked to see if the coast was clear and pulled Jean's lifeless body out of the car dumped her body in the bushes got back in and drove off his heart racing and hands shaking, he then noticed her handbag in the footwell he stopped the car picked it up with his hankie and looked inside he found the note from Tony about the meeting tonight and shoved it into his pocket then threw the bag into the bushes and drove off.

# Chapter 18

Thursday 12<sup>th</sup> December 1963

Norm stood at the entrance to Newsham Park he looked at his watch it was 8 p.m., it had turned very cold, and his breath gave off wisps of white clouds on the cold night air, he stamped his feet to stop them from turning into blocks of ice. He was wearing his grey pea coat and black polo neck jumper black trousers and a pair of heeled black boots. There was not a soul around which wasn't surprising they were either sitting in front of a fire or having a drink in the Newsham Park pub. He took a stroll into the park to see if she was on her way, he had no idea which house her friend lived in, he glanced at his watch under a lamplight which showed half eight, he was beginning to feel worried, where was she? After walking backwards and forwards in and out of the park he decided she wasn't going to show as it was now after nine so decided to walk home. When he arrived a little past half nine his parents greeted him with a frown. "Your home early son has Jean gone home early?" his dad asked. "Jean never turned up I waited for an hour it's obvious she is finishing with me and couldn't tell me to my face."

At that moment Chrissy came in from next door she wasn't seeing Jimmy tonight. "What's the matter Norm?"

She could see he was upset; he told his sister about Jean not turning up, Chrissy told him she hadn't been for a dress fitting since early November, Jean was using the same dressmaker as May. "Well, that proves it then she is calling off the wedding, I'm going to bed goodnight."

Madge felt sorry for her son and told her husband and Chrissy that he was well shot of her because she wasn't good enough for her eldest son to which they both agreed.

Jimmy arrived at Tony's he felt sick, he got out of the car and vomited in the gutter, he was sweating, and his body shook. He kept his finger pressed on the bell; the door was opened by an infuriated Tony shouting bloody hell I'm coming what's the panic? He was shocked to see Jimmy he looked terrible. "Hi Jimmy, I wondered who the hell was ringing, you look awful what's happened? Come on you look like you could do with a drink."

They entered the small sitting room and Jimmy flopped down in a chair and put his head in his hands which were shaking, and he began to cry.

Tony was alarmed he had never once seen Jimmy cry. "Is Jean alright?" He asked as he poured a drink and handed it to Jimmy who knocked it back in one swallow and asked for another, Tony gave him a double and asked again. "Is Jean alright? Did the old lady do the business?"

Jimmy looked up his eyes red and staring. "Jean is dead, she's dead Tony."

Tony was silent for a few minutes he was shocked he couldn't believe what he was hearing.

"Did the old bitch cock it up again? That was quick its only just turned half eight, where is she?"

"I left her in the park it wasn't the old woman I killed her it was me."

Tony was speechless, Jimmy had changed from a cocky likeable bloke who loved the good life and women to this man who had killed his mistress and his unborn child.

Jimmy told Tony what had happened earlier and asked Tony what he could do?

"Phone yours and tell your mum you're staying in mine as far as anyone knows you have been here all night, Cissy won't know she has been out, just keep mum when she is found, the coppers will think she has been attacked by a stranger it will remain unsolved, just carry on as normal go into work tomorrow see Chrissy tomorrow night come on mate you don't want to end up with a rope around your neck, when are you moving into the house?"

Tony changed the subject to get things back to normal and take his mate's mind off what he had done. "After New Year I want to spend my last Christmas at home with Mum and Dad, I'm going Christmas shopping on Saturday while Chrissy is with her mum, shall I meet you in town for a couple of pints or are you going out with Cissy?"

Tony felt relieved that Jimmy seemed his normal self now. "Yea I will meet you as long as Cissy can tag along?"

"Of course, is it serious between you two now? Is Tony the Romeo finally settling down with one woman?"

"Yea suppose so she is a lot nicer than most of the others I have known she is good fun to have around, but I have told her when we do get married, he laughed when he saw the look of shock on Jimmy's face, no more bloody babysitting for her sister, that's where she is now."

After drinking more whisky's Tony gave Jimmy a pillow and a blanket and bade him goodnight.

### Friday 13th December 1963

Jean Simmonds body was found by a man walking his dog, he immediately went to Tuebrook police station and reported his find. At 7.30 the area of the find was sealed off and the park was surrounded by police cars and the police forensic van, cars were stopped, and the drivers questioned, the pathologist confirmed that the woman had died by strangulation and the time was between 7 to 10 p.m. There had been no sexual activity. The body was taken away at 8:30 to have a post-mortem. The newspaper reporters were there and asked the police for information and were informed they were looking for a murderer and as yet they had no identification of who the young woman was.

Margaret Simmonds looked at the time on the clock on the mantlepiece Jean was usually up by now she asked her daughter Jennifer to go and wake her sister up. Today Margaret was going to ask Jean if she was pregnant, they had a good mother-daughter relationship and she felt upset to think her daughter could not confide in her.

Jenny appeared with a frown on her face. "Mum, she isn't there her bed looks like it hasn't been slept in."

"Oh, that's strange unless she got up earlier."

"Maybe she stayed out all night with Norm somewhere," Jenny smirked. "I don't think so Norm wouldn't ask her to do that, and you can take that silly grin off your face, I will pop into Woollies during my lunch to see if she went to work."

The police were still in the park they were searching for a clue to the woman's identity, the Detective Sergeant in charge had told the officers to look for a handbag, it was unusual for a woman not to have a handbag with her and that it might be thrown somewhere by her attacker, they had been informed that the deceased woman had been eight to ten weeks pregnant and there had been no evidence of rape occurring so we're looking at robbery with violence. The news of the murder spread, and people were shocked. Margaret heard about the body being found and was worried when lunch time arrived, she fled across town to Woollies to see if her daughter was in work, she approached the make-up counter to find Jean was not there.

"Excuse me, she asked one of the assistants, has Jean been into work today? Is she on her lunch break?"

A woman who was smartly dressed and her make-up applied immaculately turned and asked Margaret. "Are you her mother? I'm surprised at Jean she is normally a good timekeeper where is she?"

"I don't know where she is, she never returned home last night."

Margaret had a bad feeling and began to cry; the supervisor took her to her office at the back of the store and sat her down and gave her a drink of water. "I'm sorry Mrs Simmonds does she normally stay out. I know she is engaged perhaps she is with her fiancé?"

"No, I know she was meeting him last night but I'm sure he wouldn't keep her out."

After recovering she told the supervisor she would go home to see if she had returned.

Jimmy had gone home changed his clothes and had gone to work, he felt tired he hadn't slept he kept on seeing Jeans eyes staring every time he closed his eyes when he had managed to sleep, he was jolted awake by nightmares of Jean.

"Hey, Jimmy I have just been to a client who told me a woman's body has been found in Newsham Park, they say she was strangled but they don't know who it is yet, I heard their searching for a handbag, it's unusual for a woman not to have a handbag isn't it? Especially a young woman."

As his colleague carried on Jimmy's thoughts whirled It's a good job, I took that note out of the bag, bloody hell I will have to get it out my coat pocket in case it falls out. "Well, what do you think?"

"Sorry Fred I was just thinking of something what were you saying?"

"I asked do you think she was attacked for sex or robbery? I mean fancy walking through that park on your own, most probably sex she has screamed, and he has done her in."

"Yea your most probably right Fred."

It was now 1 p.m. and a young, uniformed police officer picked up a handbag with a plastic glove. "Over here Sir, I found this in the bushes."

The find was about half a mile from where the body was found, the DS in charge opened the bag and searched through the contents. "It wasn't robbery, here is her purse with a five-pound note and three shillings and sixpence," he also found an address book with her name and address and a photograph of herself with a man.

"OK, thank you constable get that down to the station. I will have to go and inform her parents, does anyone know if she had jewellery on her?"

"Yes Sir, she had an engagement ring and a necklace."

Arthur Makin was on duty at Westminster Road police station they had heard about the body being discovered and were waiting to hear who the victim was. Arthur had a funny feeling he knew who it was he had heard the description around 21 to 25, five foot seven, auburn hair and hazel eyes, she was wearing a red coat knee length boot and a black mini skirt Jean normally wore clothes like those and she had auburn hair, but, the one thing that puzzled him he heard she was pregnant and Norm hadn't mentioned Jean being pregnant. He was on the front desk and the phone rang he answered it he listened he now knew it was Jean, he replaced the receiver and informed his sergeant they had found a handbag and now knew the identity of the dead woman. He was shocked who would kill Jean? What was she doing in the park at that time? He felt sorry for his long-time friend Norm.

Detective Sergeant Price and Constable Brown rang the bell on flat one Victoria Terrace Bootle, this was the part of his job he hated most telling parents their daughter had been found murdered. The door was opened by Jennifer Simmonds, Jeans' 14-year-old sister, her face turned white when she saw the uniformed policeman on the doorstep, she asked them in and as they entered the sitting room Margaret looked up and screamed. "It's her it's my Jean they have found?" she began sobbing and moved backwards and forwards in the chair shaking her head. Constable Brown asked Jennifer into the kitchen and asked if her father was in work. "No, he left years ago I have a brother in the merchant navy, are you sure it's my sister?"

"I'm sorry it is we found her handbag, could you make your mum a cup of strong tea with plenty of sugar for shock then ask a neighbour to come in she will need someone with her to identify the body."

"I will do it officer. I will go with Mum."

She made three cups of tea and took then into the sitting room her mum was leaning over with her hands covering her face and the Detective Sergeant standing by the chair with his arm draped around her shoulder, he took the cup of tea he was offered. Margaret looked up at her daughter as she took the well sweetened tea, her eyes were black where her mascara had run and gave a slight smile. "Are you ready to answer some questions Mrs Simmonds?" asked DS Price, his voice full of symphony, Margaret nodded.

"When did you last see Jean?"

"Last night about half six, she was going out to meet her fiancé Norm which is short for Norman."

Constable Brown stood by the door and was writing in his notebook. "Did she mention where she was meeting him?"

"No, I assumed she would be going to his house, she hasn't been well recently I asked her to ring him and ask him to come here."

"Did you know she was pregnant?"

"I had my suspicions, but I was waiting for her to confide in me."

"Was the baby her fiancés Norm?"

"It must have been she wasn't that kind of girl what are you trying to imply?"

"Sorry Mrs Simmonds we have to ask those questions, what is his full name and where does he live, we need to speak to him as part of our enquiries."

Margaret told them then asked. "You don't think it was him? He is a lovely man who is a gentle soul he adored her and couldn't wait to marry her; they were getting married in May he will be devastated."

"Are you ready to accompany us to the mortuary to identify her body and her belongings? Who would you like to go with you?"

Constable Brown told his boss her daughter wanted to go with her, "Are you sure it's not a very nice experience for a young girl."

"Yes, I want to say goodbye to my sister."

# Chapter 19

Chrissy was walking towards the bus stop on her way home from work, it was just after five and she was looking forward to seeing Jimmy later. She saw the newspaper headlines on a stand outside a shop.

## Woman's body found in park identified!

Chrissy thought what a horrible way to die getting murdered, everyone in work was talking about it the body had not yet been identified then. When she approached the Terrace there were neighbours out of their houses looking towards the end, one neighbour asked Chrissy why were the police at her house?

"I don't know Mrs Jones I have just finished work excuse me."

She ran towards her house and ran indoors where she was met by her mum who looked strained, there were two strangers one in a police uniform and an older man who wore a long grey overcoat and wore a hat.

"Mum, what's the matter? Has anything happened to Norm or my dad?"

Gerry was sitting at the kitchen table with his mouth open looking at the policeman. The man in the long coat turned and smiled. "I'm Detective Sergeant Price and this is police constable Brown, we want to ask your brother some questions miss?"

"I'm Chrissy Bennett, Norm's sister, why do you to ask him questions?"

Her mum had tears in her eyes. "Sit down Chrissy, the police want to know when your brother last saw Jean, it was her body they found in the park."

Chrissy was struck dumb, at that moment they heard the front door open and her brother and dad talking in the hallway as they took off their coats, as they entered the kitchen their smiles froze when they saw the uniformed policeman and the plainclothes man.

"What's going on?" they both asked at once. "Hello Mr Bennett, we need to take you to the station and ask you some questions."

"Why? What questions?"

"I'm sorry to have to inform you that your fiancé Miss Jean Simmonds was found dead in Newsham Park this morning she had been strangled and we believe you may have been the last person to see her."

Norm felt his legs go and almost fell to the floor, his dad moved swiftly to stop his son from falling, Chrissy ran and got him a glass of water and handed it to her brother whose hands were shaking. After waiting for him to recover the DS asked Norm to go with them to Tuebrook police station for questioning.

"But I didn't see her last night she never turned up."

"OK Mr Bennett you can tell us what happened later."

His dad asked them if he could go with them. "I'm sorry sir but that won't be possible we will keep you informed if we need to keep him in overnight."

They left the house and put Norm into the back of the police car, the neighbours were all out looking, Maud Makin went to her friend and neighbour and led her inside, May told everyone to go back indoors then followed Chrissy inside. Gerry was being comforted by his dad. "Why have they taken our Norm, Dad? Do they think he murdered Jean? I know he wouldn't do that."

As the police car was leaving Northumberland Terrace Arthur was walking towards home when he saw Norm in the back of the police car he frowned, I hope they don't think it was him who murdered Jean because they were barking up the wrong tree Norm wouldn't hurt a bloody fly.

DS Price and another plainclothes officer were sitting at a table facing Norm, there was a uniformed officer standing by the door of the small room they were in. DS Price introduced Detective Inspector Baker to him. "OK Mr Bennett or can I call you Norman."

"I'm usually called Norm."

"Norm, can you please tell us the last time you saw Jean Simmonds?"

"I told your colleague earlier I didn't see her last night, she didn't show up as planned so the last time I saw her was Wednesday night at her mum's, she asked me to meet at 8:00 by the park because she was going to see a friend who lived in a flat in the park."

"Did you know she was pregnant? About eight to ten weeks."

Norm was shocked, that was why she hadn't turned up to the dressmakers. "No, if she was then it wasn't mine."

"She was nearly three months and showing surely you must have noticed? How do you know it wasn't yours?"

"I know because we never had sex."

The two men looked at each other with surprise and incredibility. "You're telling us you were engaged but never had relations."

"Yes, I maybe old fashioned but I was waiting till we were married."

"Ok, Norm very noble of you, what did she say to you the night before besides she was going to meet a friend."

"That was all, oh, yes she told me she had something to tell me I asked her to tell me then she asked me to wait till the Thursday."

"What do you think it might have been she was going to tell you?"

"I thought she was going to cancel the wedding; her mood had changed lately now I know why she must have been seeing someone else."

DI Baker took over the questioning.

"What time did you leave your house."

"About half six."

"How long does it take for you to walk to the park? If you walked."

"About half an hour if I walk fast."

"Why did you leave so early if you were meant to be meeting at 8, where did you go before you met her?"

"I walked slowly I had a lot on my mind."

"How long did you wait for her to turn up."

"I waited an hour it was freezing so I walked in and out of the park to see if she was coming, I didn't know what house it was only it was near the entrance."

"Did you see anyone else while you were waiting for her."

"No, it was quiet I saw a couple leaving the pub just as I was heading home."

"Weren't you worried about her? Didn't you wonder where she was? After all, she was your fiancé you say you loved her, I wouldn't leave my young woman to walk through the park alone."

"I just thought she had already returned home, or she was still in her friends and didn't want to tell me to my face we were over."

"I still find it strange you didn't bother to find out if she had returned home."

"I never thought at the time to go to her house and ask, I had waited an hour I was cold, and I was a bit annoyed she couldn't tell me to my face."

DS Price took over the questioning. "According to Miss Simmonds mother she never mentioned going to a friend's house. Only that she was meeting you,

122

she was surprised about the friend she didn't think her daughter had a friend who lived there, did you ask the friend's name?"

"No, Jean had many friends I never thought to ask."

"We have looked though her address book it shows friends living in Bootle, Waterloo and Anfield it has your name and address but no one living in the park, so why would she suggest you meet her there? Was that her idea or was it yours?"

"It was her idea."

DI Baker looked at his watch which showed 7 p.m.

"Have you had anything to eat?"

"No, I didn't have time before I was brought here can I go home now sir?"

"Not yet Norm we will break now and give you something to eat and drink."

He turned to the constable and told him to go the canteen and bring him something to eat, he left the room.

"We need to question you further Norm and then make enquiries and see if there are any witnesses who saw you leave the park and if anyone one living in the area knew Miss Simmonds so we will be keeping you in overnight."

"Oh, can't I come back tomorrow morning my family will be worried."

"Don't worry we will inform them what is happening, have a good rest and we will continue tomorrow morning."

The two detectives left the room talking quietly to each other.

After Norm had been taken away Chrissy made the tea for the family her mum was upstairs with her friend Maud trying to calm her down, Chrissy took some food to her mum but was told she didn't want anything to eat, she returned downstairs and dished out the scouse and some bread, but no one was in the mood for eating. Arthur had called in and told them he was surprised Norm was under suspicion but told them not to worry they were only questioning him now. Chrissy had phoned Jimmy's and asked to speak to him they were due to be going out to the Mardi Gras, but she couldn't go now, his mum had answered and told her Jimmy hadn't returned home yet but would ask him to ring her later. May told Chrissy she would cancel her date with Gary, but Chrissy told her to carry on as normal because she was sure Norm would return home soon.

Later Norman Bennett replaced the receiver at Maud's house thinking it was time to have their own phone put in he thanked her then went back to his and went straight upstairs to his wife who was in bed.

"That was the police Madge they are keeping him in custody overnight they want to question him again tomorrow."

"They should be out looking for the man who murdered the lass instead of keeping our son in, our Norm wouldn't hurt a fly do they think it's him?"

"They are just asking him questions it's their job once they have finished, they will let him go."

Chrissy had told Jimmy when he phoned about Norm being taken away for questioning and could they miss going out later, he had sounded shocked and told her he understood, and they would let her brother go. He told her he would meet her in town tomorrow. When her dad returned from downstairs and told her about Norm being kept in, Gerry who had been reading his comic looked up with unshed tears sparkling in her eyes. "Are they arresting him dad?"

"No, Gerry they just want to ask him more questions, he won't be arrested."

Jimmy went to meet Tony he needed to tell him about Norm he never thought the police would take him in for questioning. When Jimmy told his parents, they were shocked to learn it was Jean who had been murdered, although they hardly knew the young woman it was still upsetting that a young woman's life had been taken and that she was pregnant. Albert asked Jimmy. "Are you sure it wasn't Norm? She may have been having another man's baby and Norm lost his temper."

"No dad, he hasn't got a temper he is meek and mild I'm quite certain it wasn't him."

When he met Tony, he took him aside and told him about Norm. "I'm worried mate I never thought he would be under suspicion she was meant to be meeting him, I just hope they don't think it was him, I don't know how I am going to face Chrissy knowing it was me."

"Jimmy, stay calm he is only being questioned once they realise it wasn't him, they will let him go murder unsolved, don't go and bloody confess, come on let's have some drinks and get pissed."

### Saturday 14th December 1963

Norm had had an uncomfortable night lying on the hard bench with a thin blanket covering him. The cell door was opened by an older police sergeant. "Come on young man here is your breakfast."

"I need to go the toilet and wash my hands and face I feel dirty."

"OK, I will take you but don't take too long your breakfast will get cold and you need that before the DI and DS start questioning you."

"What time is it?"

124

"It's seven o' clock come on hurry up."

8.00

Norm was taken back to the same room where he sat and waited, the same constable as last night once more stood by the door, the door opened and a man with a briefcase entered he was short had a shiny balding head and wore small round glasses which hung on the top of his small stubby nose, his suit was blue and was worn and had seen better days. He held out his hand. "Hello Mr Bennett, I'm your solicitor Jeremy Tindall," he smiled showing yellow teeth.

"I never asked for a solicitor, who sent you? I don't need one."

"I'm the duty solicitor the police asked me to represent you while they are questioning you, now tell me what you told the police last night."

After explaining to Mr Tindall what he had told the police, Mr Tindall smiled and told him unless they charged him, they would have to let him go.

The door opened again, and Di Baker and DS Price entered the room they smiled at Norm and shook hands with Jeremy Tindall, they then sat and once more asked him the same questions as before, Jeremy Tindall interrupted and told them unless they had reason to charge him, they would have to let him go.

"We know Jeremy but we can hold him for longer as you will know this is murder a young woman and her unborn baby callously murdered and threw in the bushes, we are still making enquiries about this friend Miss Simmonds was supposed to be meeting, we are still asking people who live in the flats if they knew her and asking if anyone saw Mr Bennett enter or leave the park it takes time, we have taken your statement Mr Bennett would you read through it with Mr Tindall if it's true then please sign it."

"How long will I have to stay, my family will be worried, I haven't murdered her."

"As we explained we can keep you for a lot longer while we still carry out our investigations, the constable will take you back to your cell till we have decided whether or not to charge you."

Norm looked at them in shock. "Charge me? I have just told you; I haven't murdered Jean! I loved her."

Arthur went to Tuebrook station to enquire about Norm for his parents, he didn't know the desk sergeant. "Hello sir, my name is police constable Makin I'm a friend of Norman Bennett who is being held here, I'm just enquiring on behalf of his family how much longer he is being held."

Sergeant Johnson who had been on the force for thirty-five years was an old-fashioned man who believed in capital punishment for murder looked down at the young man before him. "Mr Bennett is being questioned in connection to the murder of Miss Jean Simmonds, he is being held until they are satisfied it wasn't him, that is all I'm telling you constable Makin I advise you to keep your nose out of this investigation it's being dealt with by two senior officers who have a very good reputation so go back home and tell his family he is still under investigation."

Arthur felt embarrassed the Sergeant had basically told him to keep out of it and not in a very nice manner.

# Chapter 20

Chrissy met Jimmy after being persuaded by her mum to carry on as normal. "I'm sure our Norm will be released later."

Chrissy and her mum were meant to have gone Christmas shopping there were only ten days left but her mum hadn't felt up to it so asked Chrissy to get the presents for her dad. Chrissy and Jimmy had finished their Christmas shopping and had arrived at Yates wine lodge which Chrissy hated on sight, it wasn't her type of pub, they were meeting Tony and Cissy so what did she expect? Jimmy noticed her look of distaste and told her they wouldn't be staying long.

"I think you have been spoilt being taking to all those clubs and restaurants," Jimmy teased.

After Tony introduced Cissy to Chrissy, she was surprised she was totally different to his usual girlfriends who were normally tarty or too young.

While Tony and Jimmy were in deep conversation Chrissy asked Cissy how long she had known Tony. "Just over two months I live with him permanently now, I have seen him around the pubs by me for years and have always fancied him, I couldn't get his attention till his girlfriend died an abortion that went wrong I heard, I saw him sitting alone and got talking then it went on from there, look at them Chrissy you would think they were twins they think the world of each other."

Chrissy looked at them with their heads close together they were close like brothers but certainly not like twins Jimmy was far better looking than Tony. She had tasted a glass of Aussie White but couldn't finish it, yuk she had said and pulled a face they all laughed. They said their goodbyes and went their separate ways. "Is Tony serious about Cissy she seems like a nice girl?"

Jimmy smiled, "I know it's unbelievable, isn't it? I wouldn't be surprised if they got hitched, shall we go back to our house before we go to mum's?"

"OK, then I will have to phone to see if Norm is home."

Once they arrived at the house, they were buying Jimmy took the shopping from Chrissy. "Come here love I want you have done most of the day."

The house was now furnished he took her upstairs into the bedroom and pushed her onto the new bed, he had just started undressing her when the phone they had installed rang out, Chrissy sat up and he pushed her back. "Leave it he rasped this is more important."

Chrissy forgot about the phone and got lost in their passionate lovemaking, Jimmy had drifted off to sleep while Chrissy lay awake, there was something different about the way he had loved her he was more demanding less romantic, he had hurt her slightly when he had been kissing her and had been a bit rough. Afterwards he held her in his arms and said he was sorry for hurting her. The phone rang again but Jimmy still hadn't stirred, so she moved out of bed threw on her coat which lay on the floor and went down the stairs and answered the shrilling phone. "Hello, its Chrissy who am I speaking to?"

"Chrissy, at last I rang before have you just got in." It was Albert. "Oh, hi Albert yea we have just got in do you want to speak to Jimmy?"

"No, love your dad rang here thinking you were here he needs you to return home as soon as you can; it's Norm he has been charged with the murder of Jean."

Norm felt tired he had been questioned again in the afternoon going over the same questions till his solicitor had asked for a break. DI Baker had carried out most of the questioning. "No one living in the flats knew Jean, her mother has told us she never mentioned going to meet a friend we only have your word she knew this mystery friend did you meet her? Did you get angry when she told you she was pregnant? After all you tell us it couldn't have been yours, so you were angry that she had been seeing someone else you lost your temper and strangled her dumped her body then her bag then ran to the entrance to the park that was the reason why you left at nine."

"No, I tell you I didn't see her I wouldn't harm her I loved her I was going to marry her for god's sake."

"You were seen by a couple leaving the park in a hurry and looking behind you."

"Suppose I did leave in a hurry I had been waiting for an hour I just wanted to get home."

"You say you loved her, yet you go home without checking if she is alright, or maybe you knew where she was because you had just left her in the park strangled."

It was now lunchtime, but he couldn't eat the meal he had been given he just drank the weak tea. The cell door opened, and the sergeant asked him to follow him to the front desk, DI Baker and DS Price were there. DS Price looked solemn then he spoke. "Norman Alan Bennett I am charging you with the murder of Miss Jean April Simmonds on the night of Thursday 12th December 1963, you will be appearing before a judge for a plea and management on Monday 16th December you will be held at Walton prison till then have you anything to say?"

"You have the wrong man. You have no proof that I am guilty where is Mr Tindall shouldn't he be here now?"

"He is with another prisoner now he will see you later to advise you on your plea."

"What about my parents will you tell them can I see my dad please?"

DI Baker looked at him, "we will inform them of what is happening we will let your father see you before we transfer you to Walton, take him back to the cell sergeant."

Chrissy ran up the stairs the bed was empty, she could hear Jimmy singing in the bathroom and dashed in he was towelling himself dry his lithe muscular body gleaming with water his dark hair tousled. "Hi, love where have you been?"

"I went to answer the phone while you were asleep, it was your dad he rang before, but we ignored it, my dad rang yours to tell us Norm has been charged with murdering Jean, he wants me home as soon as possible."

Jimmy was struck dumb, bloody hell he thought I never thought they would charge Norm stupid idiots.

"Jimmy, please hurry up."

They drove to Chrissy's in silence both too stunned by Norm being charged to think about small talk, once they arrived Chrissy jumped out of the car and ran into the house Arthur was there with May, Gerry was sitting on the floor sobbing while Arthur tried to console him.

"Mum is upstairs with her, May told Chrissy, your mum fainted when she heard the news about Norm."

"Your dad has gone the police station to see him before he is transferred to Walton prison, he had already left otherwise I would have taken him," Arthur told her.

Chrissy ran to the bedroom where Maud Makin was sitting in a chair by the bed while her mum lay asleep on the bed, Maud jumped up and took Chrissy into her chubby warm arms and they both wept.

Chrissy in her worried state had completely forgot about Jimmy, he followed her into the house and was dismayed to find Arthur there. "Hi Jimmy," May greeted him. Arthur just nodded.

"I can't believe they think Norm would murder her," Jimmy told them to break the gloomy silence.

Gerry looked up his eyes swollen his face streaked with tears. "Norm is my brother who is kind, and he wouldn't kill anyone, they have made a mistake haven't they Arthur?"

Arthur looked ashamed; he thought the same himself his colleagues had certainly got this wrong.

## Monday 16th December 1963

Norman had appeared before the judge to make his plea and to decide if they were going to trail him by the crown court, he had pleaded not guilty, and his solicitor had asked if he could be bailed but was turned down because of the severity of the charge. Because of the Christmas and New Year holidays the trial would be held in St Georges Hall on 3rd January 1964. He was to be held in Walton prison till the day of the trial, he was led away, and he told the judge that he was innocent. His dad, Chrissy and Arthur were there and were devastated, his mum was still in a state of shock and was being taken care of by her friend Maud. Arthur had brought a car and drove them home and told them Norm needed a better solicitor who would get them the best defence lawyer.

"Norm asked me to take some money from his savings but I'm not sure it would be enough," Norm's dad told them.

"Don't worry, Dad. I have some savings as well he can have."

"No, Chrissy they are for your wedding, I have spoken to your uncle Joe, and he told me he would give us the amount we might be short of, but thanks Chrissy."

When they arrived home, Gerry was there. "It's a bit early for you to be home from school, what have you done to your face?"

Gerry had a nasty scratch and a bruise on his cheek.

"It was a fight, Dad, some boy said my brother was a murderer, so I hit him."

Madge came in from the kitchen and told them the school had rang to ask to bring Gerry home they are breaking up soon so he might as well finish now, she looked ill she had bags under her eyes through lack of sleep she walked with a stoop and her hands shook.

"Gerry, you go upstairs and get changed then stay indoors we don't want you getting into more fights, are you ok?"

"Yes, Dad Christmas will be lousy this year I don't want presents I just want my brother back home."

When Gerry had left the room, Madge sat down with a big sigh. "If he is found guilty, he will be hanged." It was said with such calmness with such finality they could not respond.

Jimmy had taken a day off work how could he concentrate while he had this guilt eating away inside of him. The phone rang interrupting his thoughts his mum answered. "Jimmy, its Chrissy."

He replaced the receiver and stood in the hallway he felt sick, Chrissy had just told him the trial was on 3rd January.

"Are you feeling alright Jimmy your looking pale what did Chrissy have to say?"

He told his mum about the trial, "They must think it's him, he must have done it or they wouldn't have charged him."

He shook his head, "No, Mum. I'm sure it wasn't him he is not violent he wouldn't hurt anyone much less murder them."

# Chapter 21

**3<sup>rd</sup> January 1964**

3<sup>rd</sup> January 1964

Chrissy lay awake it was the day of the trial she had hardly slept and had heard her mum crying. Christmas had been a terrible time no one wanted to celebrate, they had stayed in Southport. Chrissy had seen Jimmy on New Year's Eve and had spent it in the new house with Tony and Cissy, they had left early because she and Jimmy had felt so miserable. Chrissy got up and got washed and dressed, she had decided on a black skirt, white blouse and a warm cardigan she wasn't sure how warm St Georges courtroom might be. Her dad was up making breakfast. "Morning love, do you want a bacon, buttie?"

"No thanks, Dad I don't feel very hungry I will just have some toast, how is Mum?"

"Tired love she has hardly slept I told her to stay home with Maud, but she wants to go and support our Norm, I'm trying to persuade her to have something to eat she looks like she has lost weight."

Chrissy took a long look at her dad, he looked ill his face normally so healthy and pink looked drawn and white, his shoulders stooped, and it looked like he had shrunk.

"Sit down, Dad. I will make a pot of tea and finish off the bacon then take it up to Mum, its only seven, we have three hours yet."

Gerry had remained in Southport while they were attending the trial, Arthur was taking them to the court he was going to be a character witness for the defence. Norm was being represented by Henry Price-Harris QC. The phone rang her dad answered and told her it was Jimmy. "Hello love, how are you? I'm sorry but I can't make it to court today I'm unable to get time off."

"Oh, Jimmy I was hoping you would be there to hold my hand and support me."

He felt awful for upsetting her but how could he sit there in court knowing they had the wrong man, and he was too cowardly to own up, he was usually a man who overcame any problems but, on this occasion, he couldn't face seeing Norm up in the dock.

"Hello, Jimmy are you still there?"

"Yes, look I'm sorry but I need to go to work I will call around later, and you can tell me how it went."

She heard a click he had hung up; she went into the kitchen crying her dad had finished preparing a tray to take up to his wife and looked at his daughter. "What's the matter?" he took her into his arms, and she sobbed into his chest. "Jimmy has just told me he can't make it to the trial he can't get the time off work."

"You have to understand Chrissy he has to go to work to earn a wage to pay for the mortgage on the house, we will have Arthur, Maud, May and your uncle Joe to support us, come on love be strong for our Norm he needs all the help he can get."

## The Trial

Norm was woken early and given breakfast before he was taken to St Georges Hall court, he had not eaten much his stomach felt full of nerves. He was innocent but that didn't stop the police making mistakes, he remembered innocent men were still found guilty and hung. He knew of the wrong conviction and hanging of Timothy Evans although they had discovered later it was his landlord John Christie who had murdered Timothy's wife, if they could make a mistake then why not now with himself? His dad had bought his suit for him to wear in court, but it hung loosely on him and made him look gaunt. He also knew this trial would not last long his barrister had told him he had only his word to convince the judge and jury that he was innocent, he was told the prosecution only had two witnesses who had seen him leave the park, the only other defence were his character witnesses, Arthur, his old headmaster Mr Swain and his manager from the Automatic where he worked. The time arrived and he was escorted from the holding cells below the courtroom up the stairs and into the dock. He saw his parents, Chrissy, Maud. Uncle Joe sitting in the public gallery his dad gave him a little smile of encouragement, he also noticed Jean's mum and sister and a couple of his neighbours. He looked over at his barrister Henry Price-Harris QC, a towering man of huge proportions with his large nose and full lips he looked scary, but he had a very good reputation. Also, in the court room was the clerk of the court and a woman taking notes, the prosecution was led by Harvey Benedict QC who seemed relatively young to Price Harris and was rather a good looking man. The court was asked to stand, and the judge Mr Justice Harvey entered the court, then the jury of ten men and two women were empanelled.

Harvey Benedict QC made the opening address for the crown, he told the jury there were only two witnesses for the prosecution this was a simple case of deciding if this person now standing in the dock had callously strangled his fiancé who was carrying his or another man's baby.

"I would like to call to the witness box Mr John Taylor."

Mr Taylor was a man of small stature a full head of black hair and in his early thirties his occupation being a milkman, once he had been sworn in Benedict began his questioning.

"Mr Taylor can you tell the court what you saw on the night of 12$^{th}$ December last year."

"Yes sir, me and the wife had been drinking in the Newsham Park pub it was around 9:00 I had to leave early cos I was in work early the next morning, it was a horrible night there was no one around then we saw someone leaving the park in a hurry."

"Mr Taylor can you see that person in court now?"

He looked around and answered yes, he was asked to point the person out then pointed his finger at Norm. "Was he walking or running from the park?"

"Not really running but walking very quickly."

"What made you notice him it was dark and misty that night?"

"As I said there was no one else around and he wasn't that far away we could hardly miss him, my Mrs remarked that he looked a bit like Ringo Starr."

"Did he look scared because you had seen him leave the park?"

At that point Price-Harris objected, pointing out that the witness could not have known what Mr Bennett was feeling at the time. Justice Harvey agreed with Price-Harris.

The defence then proceeded to question Mr Taylor stating as it was a cold night it would not be unusual for a person too be walking quickly. The same questions were asked to Mrs Taylor who confirmed what her husband had told the court.

The prosecution also called Mrs Margaret Simmonds although she was reluctant to give evidence for the prosecution because she still believed Norm was innocent.

"Mrs Simmonds when was the last time you saw your daughter alive?"

"On the Thursday 12th December."

"Did she tell you where she was going that night?"

"Yes, she was meeting Norm." Margaret looked over at Norm and gave him a small smile.

"Did she mention she was meeting a friend who lived in Newsham Park?"

"No, she just mentioned she was meeting Norm."

"Were you shocked to learn that she was eight to ten weeks pregnant?"

"No, I had my suspicions when I heard her being sick in the mornings, I was waiting for her to tell me."

"Did you think it was Norm's?"

"Yes, I wasn't upset they were engaged I thought they would bring their wedding forward."

"I'm sorry for your loss Mrs Simmonds but I must ask you did you suspect she was seeing another man?"

"No."

"No more questions."

Price-Harris stood, "May I convey my condolences for the loss of your daughter, do you like Norm? did you think he was a good person to be marrying your daughter?"

"Yes, I do like Norm he is a good honest man who thought the world of Jean."

"Did you ever suspect she was seeing another man? She was pregnant but it was not the defendant's baby, she had not arrived for her wedding dress fitting since November."

"No, I had no reason to suspect she was seeing someone else she seemed happy with Norm she was marrying him."

"It's quite obvious she was seeing someone else and she was having a child by this other man, according to the defendant and his family and friends she had changed into a surly and demanding woman, I suggest she was meeting this other man before she met Norm, she told this unknown person she was pregnant, and he became angry and strangled her."

"No, my Jean was a good girl she would not cheat on Norm," Margaret Simmonds began to cry. Price-Harris told her he had no more questions and that she may stand down. At that point Justice Harvey called for an adjournment for lunch, the court stood, and Justice Harvey left the Court. Norm was taken back down to the holding cells and the jury and the public left.

The Bennett family and their friends went to a café near the court, Madge looked at her husband then asked Arthur when he would be called as a character witness. "I don't know Aunt Madge it could be today if the prosecution finishes their case, if not it will be tomorrow, they will call the character witnesses first then put Norm in the box."

After lunch they returned to the court and the case proceeded once more. The prosecution had finished their case and it was the turn of the defence, Arthur was called first, he gave his name and occupation then asked how long he had known the defendant.

"I've known Norm all my life we grew up together, there is only a couple of months between us, he is more like a brother to me."

"Can you please tell the court what kind of person Norm is?"

"He is a quiet serious man who would help anyone, he hates violence of any sort and if he saw a fight, he would try and break it up and calm them down, I remember he saw a man kicking his dog and he was brave enough to tell the man off for being cruel."

"Were you surprised when he started dating Ms Simmonds?"

"I must admit I was surprised they seemed so different in personalities; she was a lively what you may call a good-time girl—"

Arthur was interrupted by Harvey Benedict, "I object to that phrase he is making out that Ms Simmonds seem more like a woman who slept round, can you please rephrase your description of Ms Simmonds Constable Makin."

"I'm sorry if I have caused offence, I couldn't think of another way to describe her personality, but in the end, she was cheating on Norm and was expecting another man's baby."

"No more questions Constable Makin."

The judge asked Benedict if he had any question for Makin to which he replied no.

After Arthur, Mr Swain Norm's ex-headmaster then Mr Todd his manager gave their character statements. Mr Price-Jones told the court he would be calling the defendant to the box, Justice Harvey told the court he would adjourn till tomorrow at ten.

Jimmy called around to see Chrissy, "How did it go love?"

She took him into the front parlour. "I don't want Mum to hear it doesn't look too promising, no one seems to believe the person she was supposed to be meeting exists, Norm has no proof where he was, and he was seen rushing from the park."

Jimmy looked down he couldn't look her in the eyes. "Do you fancy coming out for a drink take your mind off the trial?"

"No, I'm sorry Jimmy I need to stay with Mum, do you mind?"

"Of course not, I understand, I'll see you tomorrow hopefully something will turn up tomorrow and he will be released."

He went to meet Tony and told him how uncomfortable he felt. "I don't know how long I can keep this pretence up mate I'm glad she wanted to stay home tonight so I don't have to listen her going on about the trial, I feel lousy if only I hadn't given in to temptation, I should have avoided Jean."

"You should have used a prossy, no emotional ties, you made a mistake in satisfying your sexual urges too close to home."

## The Trial Day 2

Norm was called to the stand, after swearing on the bible and giving his name age and occupation he felt ready to give his side of the story. Mr Price-Harris QC asked him to tell the court the events leading up to the night of Ms Simmonds murder. He told them of Wednesday night the last time her saw her and being asked to meet her the following night by the park because she was visiting a friend who lived there, he told the court how he had waited for an hour and her not turning up then returning home.

"Did you ask Ms Simmonds what she wanted to see you for? In your statement you mentioned you never usually saw each other on a Thursday."

"I did ask her, but she asked me to wait till the Thursday."

"What did you think then? Were you suspicious?"

"I thought she might be calling off the wedding I wondered why she couldn't tell me then."

"Why did you think she might be calling off the wedding? Did she give you any clues she might be?"

"I noticed she had changed she had become moody, she wasn't her usual bubbly chatty self, she started asking for things I couldn't afford, going to clubs and fancy restaurants and buying a car."

"Didn't you have any clue she might be seeing another man and she was pregnant?"

"No."

"When she didn't arrive that night, you say you waited for an hour why wait that long?"

"Yes, I wanted to give her a chance to turn up thought she might have forgotten the time, she was never on time."

"When you left the park did you run or walk?"

"I walked quickly I was cold and just wanted to get home in the warm."

"What were your thoughts as you walked home?"

"I knew then that it was over she wanted to finish with me but didn't have the decency to tell me to my face, it was only then I thought she might be seeing someone else."

"If she had told you, she was pregnant what would have been your reaction."

"I would have been shocked which I was when I found out."

"Would you have still wanted to marry her? Or would you have lost your temper and strangled her?"

"No, I loved her I wouldn't hurt anyone, never mind murder them."

Mr Price-Harris told Norm he had no more questions, Mr Harvey Benedict QC stood up he was silent for a couple of minutes while he stared hard at Norm.

"Are you always so meek?"

Norm frowned, "If you mean easy going, I suppose I am."

"No, I mean weak, submissive easily led?"

"I don't understand what you're implying."

"What I'm trying to ask is why you didn't demand to be told that night what she wanted to tell you."

"As I said I'm not that kind of person."

"You have told the court she had turned surly and demanding and you still wanted to marry her, I'm sure any man wouldn't stand for that kind of behaviour despite loving them."

"I thought she might have changed once we were married and settled in our own home."

138

"This friend she was supposed to be meeting she never existed, Mrs Simmonds has never heard of any such friend and the police could not find any person living in the flats who knew her."

"Why would I make the friend up? Why would I suggest meeting in the park?"

"She told you that night that she was pregnant, I suggest you were shocked so suggested you meet in the park to discuss what to do you met her with anger in your heart you loved her, but she had cheated on you, you argued then lost your temper and strangled her, why leave your house at that time it? Wasn't it eight that you were supposed to meet her it was earlier, you dumped her body then her bag and hurried from the park where you were seen looking back."

"No, you're wrong that's not how it happened I didn't see her on the Thursday."

"You showed no emotion when questioned by the police most people who are innocent shout and lose their temper you seem to have got over her death pretty quickly, you are a cool person to others but in reality, when hurt you can quite easily lose that cool exterior and lose your temper."

"You are wrong about me I am sorry she is dead she didn't deserve to die I didn't kill her."

Mr Benedict told the court he had no more questions, Justice Harvey then adjourned for lunch then the defence and prosecution would make their closing speeches.

After lunch when court recommenced Mr Price-Harris QC stood and gave his closing speech for the defence.

"The court has heard the character witnesses from a serving police officer who has known the defendant all his life, they have heard from a headmaster a long-serving pillar of society and his work manager an ex-sergeant who served his country in the last war, they are professional men who are you might assume are good judges of character, they all are in agreement that the defendant is a kind, honest hardworking serious man who wouldn't harm anyone much less his fiancé. You have heard of this mysterious friend Ms Simmonds was supposed to be meeting, what if this friend was a man the unborn child's father, it's not beyond the bounds of possibility that she met him earlier told him she was pregnant and he wasn't interested, is it not possible this unknown man lost his temper and strangled her. I want you the jury to keep these in mind when deliberating whether the evidence put before you leave you in any reasonable doubt that the defendant carried out this act upon his fiancé then you must find him not guilty."

Mr Harvey Benedict QC then stood. "I ask the jury if they believe the evidence from the defendant that Ms Simmonds was meeting a friend who the police found non-existent, why didn't he demand to be told the previous night what she wanted to tell him why wait? Was it true the child wasn't his? We only have his word it couldn't have been his, if it wasn't his it was obvious, she had been cheating on him and he had met her that night and he had lost his temper and strangled her. We only have the defendant's version of the true events of the night of twelve of December. Ladies and gentlemen of the jury the defence have not proven the defendant is innocent, you must look at the evidence against and decide if the defendant is a cool unemotional liar and that he did strangle Ms Jean Simmonds and her unborn child on that fateful night and find him guilty of murder."

Mr Justice Harvey looked at the jury.

"You have heard the evidence from the two witnesses and Mrs Simmonds, the defendant admits to leaving the park in a hurry and Mrs Simmonds states her daughter never mentioned meeting a friend only the defendant You must decide if the prosecution have proved beyond all reasonable doubt that the defendant has lied about this friend and it was him who carried out this cruel act upon his fiancé then you must find him guilty."

Justice Harvey then referred to the evidence of the character witnesses and the defendant's testimony.

"While it's clear these pillars of society have given a glowing account of the defendant's character it does not necessary mean he is incapable of this crime. You decide on the evidence alone of the defendant, has he put reasonable doubt in your mind that he did carry out this crime and that Ms Simmonds did indeed meet the baby's father and this unknown person did carry out the crime then you must find the defendant not guilty."

Justice Harvey then dismissed the jury. The time was 1 p.m. and the Bennetts went to the same café as the previous day Arthur told them he would wait in court and let them know if the jury had come to a decision, if it wasn't today than it would be tomorrow. Chrissy had asked Arthur what he had thought of Norm's chances.

"I personally don't think the prosecution have enough evidence but it's up to the jury who they believe, the judge seemed to tell the jury to ignore the testimony of the character witnesses."

Chrissy wished Jimmy was with her she hadn't seen him since last evening and she missed him. After lunch they returned to the court to find the jury were still out deliberating, Norman looked at his wife she looked ill he didn't know how long she could stand this waiting, was it a good sign they were still deciding?

Then it happened it was now three thirty the usher called everyone back into the court. The judge asked the foreman to stand.

"Have you reached a verdict upon the majority agree, if yes what is the verdict? Please answer only guilty or not guilty."

"Guilty."

There was uproar in the court Madge screamed, "No, no, you're wrong."

Norm shouted, "I didn't kill her I loved her you have the wrong man."

Mr Justice Harvey bought down his gavel down on the sounding block, "Silence in court."

Norm gripped the dock rail; he was asked if he had anything to say before sentence was passed. In a low voice, barely audible, Norm answered, "I am not guilty you have the wrong man. I'm not a murderer."

The black cap feared by many was placed upon on Justice Harvey's head there was a gasp from the public gallery most notable from the Bennetts and their friends, Justice Harvey turned to Norm and in a crisp tone told him. "On the night of 12th December 1963, you committed a cruel and brutal murder for which the jury have found you guilty, Norman Alan Bennett you will be taken to the place in which you were confined and from there to a place of execution where you will suffer death in the manner authorised by law and may the lord have mercy on your soul."

Norm visibly wilted he started to cry and shouted to the judge. "I'm innocent!" Then was taken down to the holding cell below the court room.

After the jury and court were dismissed, Norman helped his wife who had collapsed, they were taken to a room where she was given a cup of hot sweet tea, when she had recovered sufficiently Arthur went to collect his car to take them home.

# Chapter 22

The Bennett family were devastated the doctor had been called out to Madge and had prescribed sedatives which made her sleep most of the time. Norman had aged dramatically he was pale faced stooped in stature and smoked non-stop, Chrissy kept remembering the look of shock on her brothers face when the judge had donned the black cap. Her brother had cried as he was led away. Chrissy had not seen Jimmy for a couple of days they had spoken on the phone and Jimmy had been shocked to hear of the verdict and sentence, she had pleaded with him to call around, but somehow seemed reluctant stating he didn't want to intrude on them at this time. Gerry had stayed in Southport to save him from the publicity he still didn't know his brother was to be hung on the 17th of February. Their barrister had told them he would appeal the sentence which would give them time to find more information he felt there were more questions to be asked from the police.

### Saturday 1st February 1964

A train pulled into Lime Street station it was 8pm in the evening, a small plump white-haired woman stepped off the train a suitcase in her hand, her hair was straggling out her bun on the back of her small round head, she blinked as the station lights shone in her tired eyes. It had been a long journey from Cornwall, and she could not wait to get back to her own home but first she would go the chippy and get some fish, chips and mushy peas and a cup of hot strong tea. Mrs C as she was known had put the parcel of fish and chips wrapped in an old Liverpool Echo on a low light in the oven while she got changed, it was while she was unwrapping her supper that she noticed the headlines in the Echo about a young woman's body found in Newsham park she had been strangled, she emptied the contents onto a plate and read the full article while she ate, something alerted her this paper was dated 14th December 1963, the description of the woman seemed vaguely familiar. She finished her supper threw the paper in the bin and went to bed the article forgotten and fell soundly to sleep.

## Monday 3rd February 1964

Norman answered the phone he looked through to the front parlour his wife was sitting just staring into space. After listening to the solicitor, he replaced the receiver with a big sigh, how was he going to relay this new shocking news to Madge, he decided to wait till Chrissy returned from work. He went upstairs and sat on his bed and cried, he got up and shut the bedroom door he didn't want his wife to hear him he had to be strong. His lovely family were torn apart, he wished Norm had never met Jean he didn't wish murder on the poor girl but someone out there was guilty, and his gentle quiet son was getting the blame and was going to lose his life.

Chrissy returned home from work her dad was in the kitchen preparing the tea, his eyes were red and swollen and his hands so usually steady shook.

"Dad, sit down I'll finish tea."

"I need to speak with you love, he closed the kitchen door, his appeal has been dismissed by the Lord Chief Justice the hanging will still be carried out on the 17th of February."

Chrissy was stunned she could not speak, she felt there was a lump in her throat that was stopping her from breathing, she had prayed the appeal would be given. "Why?"

She did not realise she had spoken out loud, her dad shrugged. "Have you told Mum yet?"

"Not yet I thought I would wait till you got home this is going to kill her."

At that moment there was a light knock on the back door and Arthur appeared he saw the expressions on their faces and slumped in the chair. "No need to ask is there? I can't believe it I wish I could do more there is more to this I'm sure there must be more questions to ask."

No one was listening to his rambling. "We will have something to eat first then tell Mum, we must get her to eat something."

"To tell the truth Chrissy I don't feel like eating either."

"Dad, you must have something. You and Mum are losing weight I need you and Mum around when the time comes, we must be strong."

After a small meal they gave the bad news to Madge as expected she went into shock and screamed, Maud came running in from next door. "Arthur has told me I will take Madge upstairs have you any sedatives left."

Later when her mum had fallen asleep Jimmy phoned. "How are things Chrissy?"

"Awful, Norm has had his appeal dismissed. Mum is in shock in bed dad is a shadow of his former self and you my fiancé seemed to have deserted me you haven't been here to support me."

The line was silent for so long Chrissy thought he had gone.

"Jimmy are you still there?"

"Sorry Chrissy, I'm in shock about Norm I didn't want to intrude be in the way."

"You won't be, Jimmy. I need you here, Jimmy. I miss you so much."

"Ok, I will be there in an hour."

He replaced the receiver and stood in the hallway; how can I face her? He thought, his mind was in turmoil he wanted to see her he wanted to hold her in his arms make love to her, but he was afraid his eyes would show his guilt. Over an hour later he knocked on the door Chrissy answered the door and she fell into his arms crying he let her cry on his shoulder he was wordless what could he say?

Chrissy lifted her head and looked at him and gave a small smile. "I have missed you so much come in let's go into the front parlour."

"Where is your mum and dad?"

As she led him into the front parlour, she told him her dad had woken her mum and asked Arthur to take them to Southport to recover her dad was staying overnight and would be returning home tomorrow. Once in the parlour Chrissy went into his arms and kissed him, he was reluctant she felt his resistance and pulled back looking at him with a frown on her tear-stained face. "What's the matter Jimmy? You would normally take advantage of us being alone don't you love me now? Do you think my brother is guilty and you don't want to be with a murderer's sister?"

He was shocked to hear what Chrissy thought. "Of course, not I love you I don't believe Norm is guilty I just don't know what to do or say to you."

"Love me then."

She took him by the hand and led him upstairs to her bedroom, at first, he hesitated but when he saw her naked body and the wanting in her eyes, he made love to her with a passion that left them both breathless. Much later after making love again he woke her up. "I must go now, love. I don't want to fall asleep and be here when your dad returns although I would love to remain with you all night."

"I feel guilty for thinking about myself, but I can't wait till we get married, I don't want a big wedding now I don't think Mum and Dad will be ready for a big celebration and neither will I. Would you mind if it was a quiet wedding or am I being selfish thinking like this while my brother is waiting to go to his death?"

Jimmy didn't answer.

## Tuesday 4<sup>th</sup> February 1964

Mrs C was visiting her long-time friend Edna and was showing her photos of her grandson, Edna was tying up bundles of old newspapers for her husband to use in his allotment when Mrs C noticed a headline with a picture about the murder in the park.

"Hey up Edna let's look at that paper."

Edna looked surprised then said, "Of course you have missed all the news about that murder." She then handed her friend the paper

After reading the article Mrs C looked up and told her friend. "That's not the bloke who murdered that woman."

"How do you know?"

Mrs C told her friend about the couple who had turned up at her house so she could abort the young woman's pregnancy, her friend knew she carried out abortions.

"What makes you think it's not him."

"Because the bloke she was with was cleanshaven and he was very handsome, that one, she said pointing at the photo in the paper, has a moustache and has a larger nose, it's not him."

"What are you going to do? you need to inform the cops they have the wrong man the poor bugger is going to the gallows soon."

They were both silent they knew if Mrs C went to tell the police she would be prosecuted for carrying out illegal abortions. After an hour of discussing Mrs C's dilemma Mrs C told her friend she would take a chance and inform the police, she would tell them they had called at the wrong house.

That afternoon, around 4 p.m., Mrs C was to change the lives of two families, she walked into Tuebrook police station and asked to speak whoever oversaw the woman in the park murder. The desk sergeant looked down on this small old lady and smiled. "Why do you want to speak with them Mrs?"

With a glint of defiance in her eyes and her head held high she told the sergeant she would tell the ones in charge and would he please tell them right away.

The sergeant having been told to do as she asked walked away with a smile on his face wondering why a little old lady would want to speak to them about.

The detectives who had charged Norm with the murder called Mrs C into a small room with a small table and four chairs. "Please sit down, Mrs…?"

"I'm known as Mrs C who am I speaking to?"

"Sorry I'm Detective Inspector Baker and this is Detective Sergeant Price."

They both looked at Mrs C and smiled, DI Baker spoke first. "What do you want to speak to us about Mrs C?"

"That young man who is going to be hanged for the murder in the park is innocent you have got the wrong man."

Their smiles faded, "What makes you think that?" DI Baker asked.

"I don't think it I know it's not him, because on the night of the murder the young woman arrived at my house with her young man asking for an abortion, I was shocked and told them they had the wrong house I don't do things like that they must have been given the wrong address and sent them on their way but not before I had a good look at them from the light in my hall, the man with her was cleanshaven he was better looking handsome even and his nose wasn't as large as the man in the Echo."

They shifted in their seats uncomfortably. "Why has it taken you so long to come forward we asked for witnesses to come forward?"

"I have been away visiting my daughter in Cornwall and only returned three days ago when I saw the story in an old Echo."

"What time did they arrive at your house?"

"Seven o'clock the night of the murder."

"Are you sure it was the same night as the murder?"

"Yes, I have just said haven't I I'm not senile, yet you know, it was the night before I left for Cornwall."

"You definitely got a good look at the man it was dark?"

"How many times must I tell you I saw him clearly I had the hall light on he was well dressed very tall and had dark hair very handsome man I thought at the time."

The DS and DI both stood, "We will get someone to give you a cup of tea we might have to keep you here a little longer will you be alright with that?"

"Yes, anything to help the young man."

They went into their superintendent's office and told him about the new evidence that had just arrived regarding the murder in the park case, he scowled. "Am I hearing this right? So, you have condemned the wrong man? I don't want you two to deal with this new evidence."

He picked up the phone and asked for Detective Inspector Morris and Detective Sergeant Dunn to come to his office immediately, he looked at his two detectives. "If this witness is correct and we have charged the wrong man we will have to postpone the hanging as soon as possible and investigate the whole case again, we know you will be punished for this the public will lose confidence in us, get out now."

After the two new detectives were briefed, they took a statement from Mrs C whose real name was Mrs Agnes Clarke and asked her to describe the man who accompanied Ms Simmonds, they then spoke to Norm's solicitor and informed him of the new evidence. He told them he would contact Mr Price-Harris to get the hanging postponed. They went to the Bennetts home to inform them of the new evidence.

It was now seven o'clock they knocked on the door and Chrissy answered and saw two men in dark suits standing on the doorstep.

"Hello," one of them smiled. "My name is Detective Inspector Morris, and my colleague is Detective Sergeant Dunn." They showed her their ID's. "May we come in?"

"Yes of course." Chrissy led them into the back room where her dad was sitting by the fire reading his paper.

"Dad, these are detectives Morris and Dunn they want to speak to us."

Norman stood and shook their hands, "would you like a cup of tea?"

"Yes, please that would be most welcome it's chilly out."

When they had drunk their tea, Norman asked them if there was anything wrong. "It's not my son is it is he alright? I know he isn't coping well."

"No Mr Bennett, can we call you Norman and…" They looked at Chrissy.

"My name is Chrissy his sister."

"Norman is fine."

"Norman, Chrissy you will find its good news, earlier today a woman came into the station claiming the man who was with Ms Simmonds on the night of her death was not your son, it seems Ms Simmonds and this man called at her house asking for an abortion."

There was a loud gasp from Norman and Chrissy, she flopped down in the chair and Norman stood with his hands over his face.

"Norman, can we ask where Mrs Bennett is so we may ask her some questions with you and your daughter they were not asked at the original investigation because they were not relevant at that time."

"My wife is very ill sir she is on sedatives and is staying in Southport with my sister."

"That's OK Norman, we won't bother her, we know your son told the other officers he left here at 6:30 was it exactly that time maybe earlier."

Chrissy answered, "I remember the scene at 6:30 was on the telly I was watching it with my mum it was just after it started when Norm came in to say goodbye. Mum can confirm that I think Dad was in the kitchen with our Gerry."

"I can't remember exactly when, but he popped his head in to say goodbye and our Gerry kept him a bit longer asking about the game sorry I didn't notice the time."

DI Morris rubbed his cheek and stood thinking, "I gather then he must have left after half six so that would not give him time to get to New Road in Tuebrook at seven which is the time when they arrived so with the new evidence it looks like your son is innocent."

"Sir we always knew he was innocent," Norman told them.

"Oh, Dad, it looks like he is going to be released from jail."

DI Morris shook his head. "Not yet I'm afraid of course the hanging with be postponed but we will have to fully investigate this new evidence and find the murderer only then will he be released."

The detectives bid them goodnight and told them they would keep them informed; Norman smiled for the first time in weeks. "It's looking good Chrissy shall we go to Southport now and tell them the good news it will certainly help your mum we can stay the night then bring her and Gerry home."

Chrissy wasn't so sure, "Don't you think we should wait till we have more information."

Her dad was aminated and was determined to bring his wife and youngest son home. "No Chrissy, I want them home let's go now."

"I will have to ring Jimmy first tell him not to call round."

The phone rang out for a long time there was no answer, she thought she might have missed him so called his parents' house to see if he was there, the phone was answered immediately it was Jimmy who answered. "Hi Chrissy, don't worry I was just on my way."

Chrissy told him the news again the phone went dead. "Jimmy, Jimmy are you still there?"

Jimmy's hand was shaking he felt hot and felt sick. "Yes, still here sorry I was surprised, has the woman given a description of the man."

"Yes, and it can't be our Norm because he wouldn't have had enough time to reach the woman's house, sorry Jimmy I must go. Dad is in a hurry to get to Southport I'll see you tomorrow can't wait, love you."

The phone clicked he stood there with the receiver still in his hand he replaced it then rang Tony's flat, it was a public phone in the hall so he hoped Tony would answer it first, luckily, he did. "Hello?"

"Hi Tony, are you alone?"

"I'm just on my way out with Cissy, what's wrong you sound a bit upset?"

Jimmy told Tony about the new evidence Tony swore. "Fuck, I forgot about the old biddy she was nattering on about going to Cornwall didn't take much notice thought she was going to stay now she bloody turns up; I'll make an excuse to Cissy get to mine as soon as you can."

Jimmy said goodnight to his mum and dad then drove to Tony's flat in Shaw Street, when he arrived Tony told him he had rung a contact he knew in London who would let him stay and get him a false ID and passport, then book a passage to New York from Southampton Jimmy shook his head. "I can't leave everyone I love behind I'll never get to see them again."

"Do you want to end up with a rope around your neck? It's the only way mate, I don't want to lose my best mate but its either leave the country or get hung."

Tony took Jimmy by the shoulders and hugged him. "I will come and visit you when everything has settled."

"What about my life with Chrissy? I had plans for us I wanted to take her to New York have kids give her a good life I won't ever see her again or Mum and Dad they will be devastated."

"Jimmy, your young bloody handsome if I may say so myself you will find someone else so come on where has the old carefree Jimmy gone?"

"I will have to go home and get some clothes."

"No, don't you need to get away now change your appearance grow a beard let your hair grow give Johnno some money and he will get you some more clothes from a charity shop, I know it's against your nature, but you will have to look scruffy just blend in with some of the Londoners then you can change when you get to Southampton."

"I don't have a choice, do I?"

"No, so goodbye my friend, no brother I will see you in New York one day."

They gave each other a brotherly hug then Jimmy left with tears in his eyes.

# Chapter 23

Arthur Makin was on duty when the news came in about new evidence regarding the woman in the park case as it was known to the public, there were posters of a man they wished to speak to in connection to the case, the sketch was of a man with dark hair and dark eyes smooth tanned skin with a high bridged nose, the lips were full. Arthur looked at the sketch it was a good likeness of Jimmy Cartwright. He showed it to his sergeant. "Sarge, I think I recognise this man."

His sergeant looked at him, "How do you know him constable Makin?"

"I think it may be Jimmy Cartwright who is engaged to Norm Bennett's sister Chrissy they are my neighbours I have known them for years."

"That sketch could look like anyone are you sure?"

"Yes, sarge I'm quite sure it's him."

Sergeant Kelly rang Tuebrook police station and told them his young colleague thinks he recognises the man in the sketch then replaced the receiver.

"OK Makin I just hope you are correct and this time we have the right man, they want you to go to Tuebrook and speak to the officers in charge, at the moment they are treating him as a witness and want him in an identity parade."

Arthur was taken in one of the police cars and while he sat in the back his thoughts turned to Chrissy, she will be heartbroken if it turned out to be Jimmy, he didn't like him but never thought he would murder anyone, Arthur had always been suspicious of him why he always seemed to have so much money, there was something dodgy about Albert Cartwright as well. His thoughts came to an end when they arrived at Tuebrook, waiting for him were DI Morris and DS Dunn. They took him into the DI's office and asked him to sit down and pushed the sketch towards him.

"OK constable Makin you say you recognise this man."

"Yes, sir it's a good likness."

"Did this person know the deceased woman?"

"Of course, his fiancé Chrissy Bennett is the sister of Norm Bennett the deceased woman's fiancé, they knew each other from school we were all in the same year together."

"Did anyone suspect they might have been having an affair."

"No Cartwright seemed very devoted to Chrissy."

"The new witness states this man who you may think is Jimmy Cartwright arrived at her house with Ms Simmonds asking for an abortion why would he be with her."

"I'm not sure about that but there was always something suspicious about Cartwright."

"In what way constable Makin?"

"He always had plenty of money even though he only worked as an insurance salesman, and he put a big deposit on a house he bought."

DI Morris and DS Dunn looked at each other in bemusement. "We don't see what that has to do with this murder just because he is loaded doesn't make him a murderer, we must be careful this time not to make assumptions in this case, but we will take his address along with his parents and any known associates we need him for an identity parade thank you for your help, constable Makin."

Arthur was now off duty, so he went bank to Westminster Road Station and drove straight home he felt tired but wanted to speak with Chrissy. "Hello, love," his mum greeted him. "Suppose you know about Norm at last they have realised they have the wrong man."

May came down the stairs and told Arthur that Norman and Chrissy had gone to Southport to give the good news to Madge and Gerry, they looked at Arthur who looked down at the floor.

"What's the matter? May asked you don't look that pleased we thought you would be happy."

Arthur took the sketch out of his pocket and placed it on the table. "Look at that sketch it's the man who was with Jean the night of her murder, who does it look like?"

May and Maud both stared at the drawing Maud put on her glasses and looked again, after a long look they both looked up and told him it looked a bit like Jimmy, but it couldn't be him.

"I wish I could show it to Chrissy."

"No, you can't do that it might not be him I know you don't like him son, but you can't be making assumptions just from one drawing."

The police knocked on the door of the house in Walton Hall Avenue it was in darkness they went around the back climbed up on the fence and saw the back was in darkness, a neighbour came out when he had put his milk bottles out and saw the police. "Can I help you officer?"

"Have you seen Mr Jimmy Cartwright the owner of this house?"

"The last time I saw him was earlier on about one he is usually home by now."

The neighbour looked at his watch which showed half 11.

"Thank you, sir, if you do happen to see him could you ask him to come down to Tuebrook police station."

"I don't think it will be tonight I'm going to bed now."

"What now?" one of the uniformed offers asked we could be here all night. DS Dunn told him they would return early the next morning if he is not at home, we will try his parents' house.

## Wednesday 5th February 1964

The police once more arrived at Walton Hall Avenue it was seven in the morning, they hammered loudly on the door there was still no reply so decided to try his parents' house. Albert and Gladys Cartwright were just having breakfast before Albert went to work, they had not heard about the new evidence. Gladys was worried. "I just hope all this upset about Norm is not going to affect their relationship they hardly seem to see each other now."

Albert was just stabbing his fork into a sausage before he could answer there was a loud knocking on their door, he looked at his watch.

"Who the hell is making this racket at this time of the morning?"

Albert went to the hallway to answer the door then Gladys heard voices in the hallway the kitchen door opened, Albert along with two uniformed police and a man in a dark suit, white shirt and black tie entered Gladys stood and looked at her husband and the intruders with a frown.

"Gladys, this is DS Dunn and constables Green and Williams they want to know if our Jimmy is here?"

"He doesn't live here no more sergeant Dunn he has his own house."

"We know Mrs Cartwright we tried there last night, and this morning can you think where else he could be, maybe a friend's house?"

"Why are you looking for him he could be on his way to work now have you tried asking them."

"Have you his firm's number I will ring the office now if I may use your phone."

Albert gave the number of the insurance company and constable Green phoned to ask if Jimmy had arrived for work, he returned to the kitchen and told them as, yet he had not arrived. "Are you going to explain why you want to speak to Jimmy?"

DS Dunn told Albert about the new witness and evidence that had come to their attention yesterday. "We just need him to attend an identity parade."

"Why?" Gladys asked. "He has been recognised from a sketch taken from the new witness's description, can you please tell us of any other friends he may have other than Anthony Marconi?"

Gladys was incensed, "So now you think my Jimmy murdered Jean, do you?"

"OK, love calm down they are only doing their job once he has been in the ID parade it will be alright."

Albert gave them the names and addresses of Ritchie and Billy.

The police had no luck with his friends, Tony had told them he had seen Jimmy yesterday, he had to tell them he had called because a neighbour had seen him. "Did he mention he was going anywhere?"

"NO."

"How long was he here for what time did he leave?"

"What's with all the questions, why are you looking for him?"

"Look we just need him for an ID parade if you happen to hear from him ask him to call in at Tuebrook police station as soon as he can, you're his best friend surely you must be wondering where he is?"

"No, I didn't even know he was missing till you turned up."

DS Dunn called in at the station to Inform DI Morris they could not find Cartwright. "He seems to have disappeared."

"Try his fiancé Miss Bennett she must know where he is, it's looking likely he might be our man if she doesn't know he has done a bunk and only a guilty man would run away."

Chrissy along with her mum, dad and Gerry had returned home her mum looked a little happier but would not be truly happy till her son was released from prison. Gerry who had been withdrawn while staying in Southport had run to his room to read his comics, he couldn't wait till his older brother was back home. Chrissy had put the kettle on when she heard a knock on the door her dad answered it. "Hello Norman, may we come in and speak to Chrissy please."

154

They entered the kitchen, and her dad introduced his wife to DS Dunn and the uniformed officer Gerry had heard them and came downstairs into the kitchen.

"Chrissy when was the last time you saw Jimmy Cartwright?"

"Monday evening." She blushed as she remembered their lovemaking.

"That was the last time you spoke to him?"

"No, I spoke to him yesterday evening before we left for Southport."

"Did you tell him about the new witness and evidence?"

"Yes of course I was happy about the news."

Her dad interrupted the questioning. "Why are you asking her about Jimmy?"

"We need to find out if Chrissy knows where he has gone."

Chrissy felt bemused by their questioning. "I don't think he has gone anywhere when I spoke to him last night, he didn't mention going anywhere he is coming to see me later I don't understand why you want to know about Jimmy?"

They explained about the description given to them by the witness and the need for him to attend an ID parade, DS Dunn took out the sketch and showed it to her. "Does this sketch show any kind of resemblance to Jimmy Cartwright?"

Chrissy stared hard it did look a bit like him she looked at the DS. "It does look a bit like him, but it could be anyone why do you think its Jimmy? Who told you it might be him? I'm sure when he arrives later, he will attend the ID parade then you can start looking for the real murderer, first Norm now Jimmy who next? My dad or even Gerry."

Gerry gasped, "I didn't do it officer honest."

Her dad told her off, "Chrissy show some respect please and stop upsetting your brother."

He looked at his wife who had earlier seemed a lot happier but now looked upset. "I must apologise on behalf of my daughter sir she was not bought up to be so rude."

"We understand Norman it's been a traumatic time for you and your family, if Jimmy arrives later Chrissy tell him he is wanted and ask him to come and see us—goodbye."

It was now after 8 pm and there was no sign of Jimmy, Chrissy had rung their new house with no answer then his parents, Gladys had sounded upset she had not seen Jimmy since the Tuesday or heard from him. Arthur was in the kitchen with May. "He is not going to turn up Chrissy it's obvious he is guilty, I'm sorry."

"Sorry, sorry," Chrissy shouted at Arthur, "your happy you have always hated him you were always jealous, was it you who gave them Jimmy's name?"

Arthur looked down, "Yes it was me it was my duty and no not jealous just suspicious, where did all his money come from Chrissy? We are investigating that and his father, Chrissy face facts he must be guilty why would he run away?"

May interrupted, "Arthur shut up please and stop goading Chrissy can't you see she is upset; he might just turn up."

Chrissy looked at her friend her eyes were shining with unshed tears, "Yes your right May, we must give him time."

Arthur went home next door his thoughts on Chrissy, no show from Cartwright, Arthur wasn't happy he felt sorry for Chrissy she deserved better he hoped he would be found and bring this whole mess to an end for the whole family.

Chrissy and May were in Chrissy's bedroom, Norman and Madge were discussing the disappearance of Jimmy.

"I think Arthur is right Madge it looks like Jimmy is guilty."

"Yes, love I can't believe Jimmy would have let Norm hang for something he hadn't done knowing he was the guilty one, he seemed such a nice honest lad who really loved Chrissy."

"I still think he does love Chrissy but for some reason got involved with Jean and got her pregnant, I'll be glad when all this is over."

# Chapter 24

Jimmy Cartwright now had a new identity his name was now David Ford, he wandered up Green Street near West Ham United's stadium he mingled with the crowd an insignificant person dressed in old grey trousers, a brown shiny corduroy jacket, dark beard and unwashed dark hair which had grown to his collar, he hated dressing like this he felt dirty, but it wouldn't be long before he was on his way to New York in three weeks' time. The attic where he was staying was damp and covered in mould and smelt of unwashed bodies and dope it made him feel ill, he stayed out as long as he could the money he had managed to take with him was running out rapidly, he had paid two hundred for a new passport fifty for a passage to New York and thirty for new clothes he kept in a suitcase in a locker at the rail station he also had to pay for meals out he couldn't bear to eat anything in the conditions he was living in. The bloke who Tony had sent him to arrange the new ID and the passport was always on the cadge for more money, he had also paid for sex because he was missing making love with Chrissy. He wiped the tears which now began to fall, and people were staring at him, it was his own fault he had ended up like this he cursed Jean but knew he shouldn't have given in to temptation. He wondered what Chrissy was thinking now, was she sad? Did she hate him? Oh god I hope not he thought, could he leave these shores and not see her or his parents and friends again?

Chrissy left work she felt tired, the constant crying was draining her energy, she felt guilty because she was jealous of May who was planning her wedding. Chrissy had cancelled the church, the hotel where they were having the wedding reception, she ripped up the invitations and sold the wedding dress which tore her heart into shreds. She wouldn't see or speak to Albert and Gladys even though she knew it wasn't their fault. Chrissy usually went home ate a little amount of food then went to her room and played records which sent her off crying again. Her parents were worried sick at the drastic change in their daughter, they told her she must eat because she looked thin, ha, she thought they will be more worried when they find out I am pregnant. At first, she thought the stress had something to do with her missed period, but when she missed two and had been sick, she knew, she was shocked and worried she had a slight bump which she hid with loose clothing, she had lost a bit of weight with not eating then being sick. Oh Jimmy where are you what have you done? Her mind screamed out.

The police had now sent out posters of Jimmy Cartwright using a photograph they had obtained from his parents. They asked airports and ferry and cruise terminals to look out for him as well. They had re-questioned his parents, friends and work colleagues and spoke to Chrissy asking her if she knew where he might be or had they arranged to meet somewhere, they had told her he had taken out money from his savings account just before he had gone missing, Chrissy had got upset and told the police she had no clue where he was and they were not meeting up and the money he had taken out was for their wedding. They had a suspicion that Tony Marconi knew more that he was telling them, but they couldn't prove anything. Arthur suggested he would keep a close eye on Chrissy in case Jimmy decided to contact her, he didn't like Cartwright but knew that he loved Chrissy and might try and see her, he was sure that Cartwright was still in the country. They gave him permission to watch her but told him to keep them informed.

Tony knew the police kept tabs on him, therefore he could not take the chance of going to London to see Jimmy, he missed his best mate and wanted to tell him the news that he Tony the Romeo was going to be a dad and at last was going to settle down with one girl. He thought of all the good times they had when they were growing up together, the scrapes and mischief they got up to, the moneymaking schemes Jimmy had always had a head for making money, he was also very popular with the girls and the older women, he remembered when Jimmy had gone to Spain with his family it was rare for working class people to travel to Spain in the fifties, it was there that Jimmy had his first sexual experience with an older woman, after that Jimmy had been like a hero to Tony. He wondered what Chrissy was thinking. He had not spoken to her since that night she had arrived at his flat asking where Jimmy was, he was shocked when he had seen her, the shy innocent Chrissy had gone to be replaced by a screaming swearing banshee, he knew he could not tell her where Jimmy was otherwise she would lead the cops straight to him and she lived next door to a copper who Tony didn't like or trust, Jimmy was better off without her. He had told Chrissy he

158

blamed her for what had happened if she had not been such a prissy goody and had let Jimmy make love to her, he would not have gone with Jean and all this would have been avoided, she had changed him and he, Tony, could not forgive her, he asked her to leave in a polite manner then shut the door on her.

## Walton Jail 12<sup>th</sup> April

Norm Bennett was at last being released he had been given his clothes and belongings and was waiting for one of the guards to take him to the gate. He had lost weight and looked gaunt and pale, three months of being locked up had hardened him up slightly he would never become a criminal but now he would not be as easy going and quiet as he used to be. Another week and he would have been hung for a crime he did not commit; he had been told by his solicitor what had transpired and thanked god and the woman for coming forward when she had and saved his life. He had also heard about Jimmy disappearing it was obvious he was guilty and to think he had once liked Jimmy and thought of him as a friend, but he was prepared to let him die by the hangman's noose to save his own neck Norm shivered at the thought. When he was let out of the big gates there was a taxi waiting for him on the other side of the road his dad stood by the taxi, not normally demonstrative in public his dad ran over to his son and took him in his arms and hugged him. "Come on son let's get you home your family are waiting."

Madge was shocked to see the change in her son but hugged him close and cried on his shoulder, Gerry stood and took his brothers hand and shook it he thought he was too big for all that soppy stuff. Norm looked at his sister the spark had left her eyes and her mouth was in a downward curve she looked up at her brother and smiled slightly then cast her eyes down to the floor she could not look him in the eyes. "Chrissy, I don't blame you for this it's not your fault don't let this come between us."

They had a salad and ham followed by ice cream it was too warm to eat anything hot, they then had a cup of strong tea which Norm enjoyed.

## London 13<sup>th</sup> April

Jimmy counted his money, he did not have enough left to keep him in New York till he managed to find work, he needed more and the only way he could get more was to contact his dad, he wanted to say goodbye to his parents but most of all he needed to see Chrissy, it was taking a risk the cops would be watching them, he had 12 days left before he left for New York. He decided to ring his dad at work and ask him to arrange something with Tony.

## Liverpool Dock

"Albert, you're wanted on the phone, it's the police." Albert walked to the office with a worried look on his face, I hope Jimmy is OK he thought have they found him?

"Hello, Albert Cartwright speaking."

"Dad?"

Albert was silent he could not talk there was someone in the office. "Dad, hello can't you speak?"

Albert asked the person if he could leave while he spoke in privacy to the police. "Jimmy, where are you son? Your mum is so worried how are you?"

"Dad I can't tell you where I am but I'm leaving the country soon and I need some more cash and to say goodbye to you, Mum and Chrissy before I go, how is Chrissy?"

"She won't speak to us or see us, son. We have tried. Norm is home from prison, it was you who murdered Jean, wasn't it? I don't agree with what you have done but we still love you, Jimmy."

Jimmy answered with a catch in his voice the tears were streaming down his changed face, unbeknown to Jimmy his dad was crying too.

"Dad I can't say too much now. Ask Tony to arrange a place where we can meet somewhere the cops won't know, do you know if they are watching you or Tony? What about Chrissy are they watching her I want you to bring her to see me, Tony will know where to go."

"I'm not sure about Chrissy I think they are watching Tony, I haven't seen them by ours, it's too risky once you get to New York me and your mum will follow you."

"Dad don't worry go to Tony then I will ring you in the Commercial pub about eight o'clock."

There was a click the phone went dead Albert stood staring at the phone Jimmy was guilty, but he still wanted to help his only son.

Albert finished work early and went immediately to Tony's flat he was glad to find him in and told him about Jimmy ringing and asking Tony to arrange a meeting. "I'm not sure if that's the right thing to do Albert it's too risky especially asking Chrissy to go with us she is a loose cannon at the moment and would alert the cops."

"He wants to see her Tony he also wants to say goodbye to me and his mam and you I have told him it's too risky he wants more cash as well, how we are going to do it without the cops getting suspicious."

"Let me have a think about it you said he is ringing later; I will meet you in the Commercial at 7:30 before he rings."

Tony met Albert and told him Jimmy should go to his house. "The cops will be watching his house Tony Jimmy wants you to meet somewhere else."

"Don't you see Albert, they won't expect him to go there they can't keep watch everywhere if they are watching me if I go somewhere else, they will get suspicious but if I go with you and Gladys to the house, they will think we are looking after it, anyway I haven't seen them lately have you?"

"No, I haven't seen any cars hanging around it's going to be hard persuading Chrissy."

"When he rings tell him to nick a car then drive-up park it anywhere then hide in the garden, they have a shed don't they. Tell him to hide in the shed, have you got spare keys for the house."

"No, Chrissy has all the keys. I don't think she has been near the house for ages."

"Ask Gladys to try and persuade Chrissy to go the house then she can open the back door tell Chrissy a neighbour has phoned to tell you he has seen a stranger hanging around the house, tell her about eight o'clock."

Albert was called to the phone. "Is that you Jimmy?"

"Yes, Dad, has Tony organised anything?"

Albert told Jimmy everything Tony had said. "I'm not sure, Dad. It seems a bit risky, but I suppose he has thought it through. I'll see you tomorrow try and get Mum to persuade Chrissy and could you lend us hundred pounds as well, bye dad."


### Tuesday 14<sup>th</sup> April London

Jimmy sneaked out of the attic he didn't want to be seen it was six in the morning and he needed to nick a car an old car so he would not be noticed then he would have time to drive to Liverpool then say goodbye to the ones he loved and most of all Chrissy, hopefully she could be persuaded to go to the house the place where he thought they would live happily with their children, how would she react when she saw him he was un-recognisable to the clean shaven well-dressed man she knew, would she still love him despite all that had happened, he missed her. After trying some cars, he found one unlocked outside a block of flats he started it up with the wires and drove off towards Liverpool, he felt happier than he had felt for a long time.

# Chapter 25

**14<sup>th</sup> April Liverpool**

Gladys waited outside the factory gates where Chrissy worked in Binns Road, Albert had told her last night what they were planning, at first, she was concerned she had told Albert if Jimmy was guilty, he should give himself in to the police. Albert had asked her if she wanted their son to hang, I'm disappointed he had an affair with Jean, but I'm sure he had not intended to kill her Albert had pointed out, Gladys agreed she didn't want her only son to hang. As Gladys waited her thoughts turned to the murder of Jean, she must have tempted Jimmy and had got pregnant on purpose to take him away from Chrissy. Gladys was upset that Chrissy had not wanted to see her and Albert since Jimmy had run away, she hoped she could persuade Chrissy to go with her to the house. The workers started to spill, from the factory gates she saw Chrissy leaving with two women and could not believe the change in her in such a short time.

"Chrissy love?"

Chrissy spun around to see who had spoken. "Gladys, what are you doing here?"

"I need to speak to you can we go somewhere?"

"There is a café up the road it will be open."

They sat at the back of the small café with a cup of tea. "How are you Chrissy love? If I may be honest, you are not looking too well."

"I'm upset and angry I thought Jimmy loved me but it seems he was a selfish man he could not wait for me to fall into bed with him so decided to cheat on me, I gave myself to him because I loved him, then he selfishly ran away to let my brother hang for a crime he committed himself, what do you want Gladys?"

"Will you meet me at the house tonight to make sure everything is OK, I can't because I have no keys and we got a message from a neighbour they had saw someone hanging around."

"I will give you the keys I don't want to ever see that house again, she paused, do you think it might be Jimmy hanging around hoping to see me?"

"No, I don't think so I need you to go with me to advise me what to do with it, it's in your name as well as Jimmy's, you can't leave it empty for much longer."

"Have you or Albert heard from him? It's unusual he hasn't contacted you knowing how much he loves you and his dad; you would tell me wouldn't you?"

"No, sorry not one word, will you meet me later at 7:30?"

"OK, but this will be the last time I will sell it and give you the money."

Arthur had been keeping watch on Chrissy but up till now she had just been going to work then going home, the only other time she had left the house was to visit his sister. His heart ached for her she looked ill, he loved her he had loved her for a long time, and he felt dishonest secretly keeping tabs on her, but he knew that Cartwright would slip up and return to see Chrissy and his parents. He knew the police were investigating other crimes he might have committed and his father Albert. He was upstairs changing out of his uniform and looked out of his bedroom window which faced onto the road he saw her leaving the house but away from his, he quickly finished changing and threw on his coat and followed her she was heading towards the bus stop, he ran back and grabbed his car keys then drove towards the stop out of sight but she was not there he then noticed the bus heading down Everton Road towards the Valley if he was right in his thinking she would head towards the valley then change buses to Walton Hall Avenue, he followed the bus and kept behind it then it stopped and Chrissy alighted then walked towards the stop to wait for another bus, he was right she was going to the house in Walton and wondered why she was going there, he waited then saw her get on to the bus then followed, at Walton Hall Avenue she got off the bus then crossed the road, he drove past and noticed there was a car in the driveway then watched as Albert and Gladys climbed out the car then was followed by Tony Marconi, that aroused his suspicions, he drove further down then got out by a telephone box.

Chrissy arrived at the house and was surprised to see Albert and Tony. "What are you doing here?" she stared hard at Tony showing her dislike for him. "I gave them a lift how are you, Chrissy?"

Chrissy ignored him, Albert approached her and pecked her cheek. "We're worried about you love can we come in with you?"

Chrissy unlocked the door remembering the last time with Jimmy she felt like screaming at them I don't want to be here without Jimmy. They entered the front room which now seemed cold and unwelcoming, she looked around the furniture had a thick layer of dust and there was a stale smell, she began to open the windows, Albert and Tony had gone out to the back garden and Gladys had put on the kettle to boil to make tea. "I've bought some milk so we can have a nice hot cup of tea and some biscuits."

"Why? I'm not staying long."

Just then the back door opened Albert and Tony entered the living room followed by a stranger. "Where did he come from who is he?" shouted Chrissy, he was tall had a scruffy dark beard and unwashed hair which was long. "What is he doing here? Get out now, have you been dossing in the shed?"

She then looked beyond the scruffy beard and hair and looked into the dark eyes with a hint of amber. "Jimmy, what are you doing here?"

Her knees buckled and she almost fell to the floor before Jimmy leaped towards her and caught her in his arms. He sat her on the black leather settee they had bought and sat beside her till she recovered. He was shocked at her appearance, her once bright laughing eyes were dull her face was pasty and spotty and her once smiling mouth was set in a downward curve, she was skin and bone he had caused this change in his darling Chrissy, and he cursed his selfishness. The others had left them alone to talk, Chrissy recovered and looked at him.

"Why are you looking like a tramp? Where have you been?"

"I need to hide my identity I won't tell you where I have been, but I am leaving the country soon I wanted to see you and my parents before I left."

"Why, Jimmy? Why did you cheat on me with her I loved you I thought you loved me?"

"I do love you I admit I have been a fool I didn't want your Norm to be hung, he won't be hung now since that woman has come forward."

"But you nearly let it happen you ran away, is that why you never came to the court why you wouldn't come to my house?"

Jimmy did not have time to answer for at that moment the door was flung open and four uniformed police officers ran in and took Jimmy by his arms and promptly clipped handcuffs with his arms behind his back. Arthur appeared with two plain clothed officers who Chrissy recognised as DI Morris and DS Dunn, but Chrissy couldn't understand why Arthur had turned up till they told Arthur, "Go on then Constable Makin you do the arrest."

Arthur had saw Tony and Cartwright's parents and had been very suspicious, why were they at the house. There could only be one reason, this is it he must be there to say goodbye to his parents and Chrissy the silly fool had slipped up. Arthur did not think for one minute that Chrissy knew he would be there, he had phoned Tuebrook station and spoke to DS Dunn about his suspicions and was told to wait till help arrived he asked them not to use their sirens to warn Cartwright they were there.

"James Albert Cartwright you are now under arrest on suspicion of the murder of Miss Jean Simmonds, you do not have to say anything, but it may harm your defence if you do not mention when questioned something which you rely on in court, anything you say may be given in evidence, take him away."

Chrissy looked at Arthur, "How did you know we were here?"

He looked down at the floor, "I'm sorry I have been following you."

DI Morris who had stayed behind said to Arthur, "Well done Constable Makin you make your statement then you can go home."

Arthur looked behind him and saw the hurt look in Chrissy's eyes he had mixed emotions, proud of his police work and felt guilty for hurting Chrissy. DI Morris looked at the people who were left. "Mr and Mrs Cartwright how long have you been in contact with your son? You do know you're in trouble for withholding information on a person on the run from the police."

"I only heard from him yesterday, my wife and Chrissy did not know Jimmy was coming here tonight."

The DI looked at Tony, "What about you I take it your Anthony Marconi?"

"Yes, that's my name and yes I knew about tonight."

"Ok, you and Mr Cartwright come with me to the station where we can question you further about this and other matters too, Mrs Cartwright and Chrissy, you may go home."

"Can we lock the house up?"

"No, Mrs Cartwright we will lock up after we have finished with our investigations into other activities your husband and son have been involved in."

Chrissy returned home refusing a lift from the police, she entered the back room where her family were watching television and promptly burst out crying, great racking sobs which shook her body, her dad jumped up and took her in his arms. "There, there what's the matter Chrissy love did you manage to sort the house with his mother?"

She couldn't speak for a long time she sat down and continued to cry her mum had gone to make her a cup of tea, but her dad gave her some brandy, Chrissy finally calmed down after drinking the soothing brandy to tell them what had happened, her dad Norm and Gerry shouted, "At last he has been arrested it's his own fault." Her mum just sat silently holding her broken-hearted daughter's hand.

DI Morris and DS Dunn sat in the small room at Tuebrook police station across the table sat Jimmy Cartwright, DI Morris started the questioning while DS Morris took down his statement. "Okay, Jimmy you know about the new evidence and witness putting you in the frame for the murder of Miss Jean Simmonds have you anything to say before we tell you of this new evidence?"

DI Morris stared hard at Jimmy; he did not reply. "If that's the way you want to play it, I will tell you, a woman came forward claiming we had charged the wrong man he paused waiting for a response non came, she then gave us a description of a man who was with Miss Simmonds on the night she was murdered asking for an abortion, was that you Jimmy?"

Again, there was no response, "Police constable Makin recognised you from the description before we had a chance to question you and ask you to take part in an identity parade you ran off, which to our minds means you are guilty is that right Jimmy?"

There was still no response, DS Dunn then began to speak. "Look, Jimmy it's no good being silent we will put you in an ID parade and she will pick you out after we have cleaned you up of course, you stink when was the last time you washed? He had a look of disgust on his long face, there are also other matters we need to ask you, you know Harold Goff? Don't try and deny it we know you worked for him on his money lending scheme, which was illegal, Jimmy nodded, well some sacks were found washed up a few miles from here can you guess what they contained?"

"No."

"At last, we are getting somewhere, they contained body parts of Harold Goff we knew it was him his wife had reported him missing a few months ago, we heard you had a big falling out with him and you your father and Tony Marconi set up your own money lending scheme which is also illegal."

"I don't know anything about Goff disappearing I left him because he was charging too much interest and he used violence to get his money back."

The two detectives looked at each other and laughed, "Too violent says the man who strangled the life out of a young woman who was carrying his child, we will continue with the questioning tomorrow and hopefully you will make our job easier by admitting to the murder."

# Chapter 26

**Wednesday 15ᵗʰ April 1964**

Jimmy was woken at six in the morning and taken for a shower and then had a shave and had his hair cut, he looked more like the handsome Jimmy Cartwright, he was then given breakfast in his cell and told to wait. At ten o'clock he was taken to a larger room with five other men they all wore overalls, and he was given a card to hold with a number four written on. Once they were all lined up the door opened and DS Dunn and a uniformed policeman entered followed by the small old lady who Jimmy remembered as Mrs C but he showed no sign of recognition, she then walked up and down the line staring into each man's face she did this a couple of times then stood in front of Jimmy and placed her hand on his shoulder as she was instructed to do, Jimmy looked into her eyes and winked at her she just tutted and shook her head. After more questioning Jimmy decided it was hopeless and the only thing, he could do now was to tell them the truth and hope for some leniency. He told them about that night and how he hadn't intended to kill her, I lost my reasoning that night he told them, he denied the accusation about the murder of Goff but admitted the accidental killing of John Jones and Ray Roach when they had asked him about their disappearance.

DI Morris shook his head, "You claim you didn't intend to kill your victims I can't believe they were all accidental murders you set out to harm them and you were not satisfied till their lives were ended, sign this statement."

He signed the statement he had refused the duty solicitor and was then charged with the murders of John Jones, Ray Roach and Jean Simmonds; he would appear before court tomorrow for a trial date, Albert and Tony were charged with illegal money lending.

Arthur was waiting at the Bennetts he needed to speak to Chrissy and tell her Jimmy had been charged with three murders and how he had earned all his money, it wasn't going to be easy despite everything Chrissy still loved Jimmy and he felt jealous. After they had eaten their tea Arthur sat her down and told her everything, she sat silent then shouted out. "No, no, no he wouldn't do that he is a caring man he loved me. still does."

Norm her brother shouted back angry that his sister still loved him, "No, he isn't a caring man he has murdered three people including his unborn child, he has made money out of people ordinary working-class people who were desperate he is not the man you thought he was, how can you still love him after all he has done and letting me your brother nearly hang, why Chrissy?"

"Because I am having his baby that's why."

There was a stunned silence, then Chrissy began to cry. "The selfish bastard," Norm shouted his parents looked shocked at Norm's outburst. "Norm we will not tolerate language like that in this house and in front of Gerry, what's the matter you have never swore like that before?"

"Mum, blame the fact I was in jail for three months, blame the fact that since he and Jean came into our lives our family has been broken." Norm then strode out of the room, and they heard the front door slam shut.

"I'll go with him and take him for a drink and calm him down." He looked at Chrissy. "Don't worry I'll look after you."

Albert and Tony went for a drink when they were released on bail, Albert could not yet face his wife and tell her about Jimmy, he felt it was his own fault for letting Jimmy return to Liverpool. They sat in the far corner in the Commercial pub it wasn't busy, so they were able to speak quietly to each other.

"I don't know why Jimmy put his hand up for Roachy it was me who shot him."

"Listen Tony he is guilty of two murders, so he decided to own up to that to keep you out of the frame he is looking out for his best friend, after all you are going to be a dad."

Tony couldn't hold back the tears that had been threatening to appear, his shoulders shook as he started to cry, Albert was surprised he had never seen Tony show any emotion before, tough Tony on the outside but he had a soft heart. Albert put his hand over Tony's then swiftly pulled it away he couldn't be seen to hold a man's hand in public.

"I will miss him Albert he has been like a brother to me I don't know how I'm going to tell me mam."

They drank till they were drunk Albert staggered home and went straight to bed he would tell his wife tomorrow. Tony went straight to bed and cried openly for his best mate.

## Wednesday 6th May 1964

The second trial for the murder of Miss Jean Simmonds had taken place, Only this time the defendant stood accused of two other murders as well, James Albert Cartwright had stood in the dock he had no defence, the prosecution had a witness for the murder of Miss Simmonds and the jury were told he had owned up to the murders of John Jones and Ray Roach, it was an easy decision for the jury to say guilty on three accounts of murder, Jimmy had pleaded they were unintentional but the fact he had run away and let another man take the blame for the murder of Miss Simmonds went against him. All that was left now was to hear what sentence he would receive. Albert and Gladys attended with Tony, Mrs Simmonds also attended she had always doubted it was Norm who had murdered her daughter, also attending was Norm. The judge told Jimmy because of his disappearance and letting an innocent man nearly lose his life left him with no choice but to impose the maximum sentence allowed by law, you have admitted to two other murders, but I must show that crimes like these will not be tolerated by society. Justice William Josephs then donned the black cap there was an audible gasp in the public gallery Gladys Cartwright was shocked she thought he would only go to prison, Justice Josephs turned to Jimmy. "James Albert Cartwright, you will be taken hence to the prison in which you were last confined (Walton) and from there, be taken to a place of execution where you will suffer death in the manner authorised by law, and may the lord have mercy on your soul."

Jimmy stood still he didn't shout or cry he looked at his parents and smiled his mum stood and ran out of the courtroom sobbing. Mrs Simmonds sat weeping, at last someone was being punished for her daughter's death, Norm just shook his head while Jimmy was led away. Justice Josephs told the court he must make an apology on behalf of the justice system for the great miscarriage of justice handed out to Norman Bennett Junior and knew without a doubt they now had the right man. Norm said thank you out of politeness but still felt aggrieved about the way he was treated; he went home to tell his family the outcome of the trial.

## Wednesday 13th May 1964

Chrissy had sold the house and decided to keep the money from the sale, the police had investigated where the money had come from to pay the deposit and found that Jimmy had been telling the truth and he did indeed get an endowment from his parents. Chrissy's mum and dad had persuaded her to keep the money to help with the baby she had decided to keep. She had received a visiting order from Jimmy that morning, her mum, dad and Norm had advised her not to go because it might be too upsetting for her and the baby. They had all come to terms with Chrissy having Jimmy's baby, she went next door to speak with May. "I can understand them not wanting me to go but I need to tell him about the baby he should know when he dies, he leaves behind another person that is part of him."

"Chrissy, you must do what you think is best for you, no one can tell you what you should do, when is it for?"

"Tomorrow afternoon."

"I will leave work early and go with you to support you."

"Oh, May thank you so much you have been so good to me even though your busy organising your wedding."

"It's what true friends do and your more like a sister."

## Thursday 14th May 1964

It was a warm day with a clear blue sky, Chrissy and May went by taxi to Walton prison in Hornby Road in Walton. They stepped out and looked up at the big imposing building surrounded by a high wall, Chrissy shivered although it was warm. "Are you OK Chrissy have you changed your mind?"

"I'm OK I still want to go I hate to think our Norm was in there he still has nightmares about the place, come on let's get this over with."

Chrissy was searched and had to leave her coat and handbag with May who was allowed to wait in the visitors waiting room. Chrissy was escorted to another part of the prison she was informed Jimmy was held in another part in the condemned cell. She sat at a table on a hard chair in a bleak room with a little window which allowed little light and warmth into the room she shivered, she looked around on the far side of the room was a door, it opened and a guard entered the room followed by Jimmy. His face lit up when he saw her and the smile she had always loved and turned her heart into somersaults still had the same effect. She smiled back despite her reservations he gulped she looked

172

radiant from the last time he had seen her; her face was glowing, and it seemed fuller. He sat opposite her. "Thanks for coming Chrissy I wasn't sure if you would, I'm sorry for all this mess you're right I was selfish."

"It's all the lies you told me as well as your cheating, how you earned your money, you used people's money problems to pay for all those good clothes you wore the car the places you took me to, I still can't believe you could kill people it's as if your two different Jimmy's."

"They were not all lies I did love you still do I came back to see you; can you ever forgive me?" His dark eyes looked intently into hers with a pleading sadness. "I don't know about forgiving you, but I know I will not forget you I will always have you in here, Chrissy pointed to her heart, there is another reason I came to see you today when you leave this life you will be leaving a part of you behind."

He looked at her with a look of bewilderment on his handsome features, then he seemed to understand what she meant.

"You're having my baby?" his eyes filled with tears there was a sob in his voice, Chrissy nodded her tears were now falling profusely which made Jimmy cry, she stood up and he noticed the slight bump. "When is it due?"

"September 10$^{th}$."

The guard told Jimmy they had five more minutes. "If it's a boy, will you call him Tony?"

"Tony?"

"Yes, after Tony Bennett."

"Ok, I will name him Anthony James."

"Thanks love, will you tell him about me when he is older?"

"Yes Jimmy."

It was time for her to leave Jimmy stood and looked at the guard. "Can we kiss goodbye?" The guard nodded Jimmy took her in his arms and kissed her hard she responded with a passion she recalled, her mind flashed back to February last year when they had first kissed, their salty tears mingled, Jimmy held on to her until the guard touched him on the arm and asked them to stop. The guard asked Chrissy to sit and wait to be escorted back then took Jimmy towards the door that was to separate them for life, he turned back to take one last look at Chrissy and once again she noticed the glint of amber in his dark brown eyes.

## Thursday 21ˢᵗ May 1964

It was eight o'clock in the morning Jimmy was in his cell he had just eaten a cooked breakfast his last meal. Suddenly a door was slammed open a secret door revealing a man who looked to be about seven foot walked into the cell, he had a cold no-nonsense look about him his eyes were as cold as ice, Follow me he asked Jimmy flanked by two officers and a vicar quoting verses from a bible he followed the man who he know knew to be the hangman, he said a secret prayer to god asking him to take care of his family, Tony, Chrissy and most importantly of all his unborn child.

## Northumberland Terrace

It was eight o'clock in the morning the terrace was quiet most people had already left for work, the weather had turned from high temperatures to an overcast sky and thundery showers which gave the terrace a gloomy atmosphere, the neighbours knew what was going to happen today and they showed respect by keeping their curtains closed. Further up the terrace an upstairs window was open the curtains blew in the brisk breeze then the eerie silence was broken by music coming from the open window and the fine tones of Tony Bennett singing. "Oh, the good life."

# Epilogue

## 13<sup>th</sup> September 1969 Cornwall

The weather was glorious for September, Chrissy lazed in the lounger in her garden overlooking the Camel Estuary. The garden had an avalanche of colours and fragrances with the African Lily, Shasta Daisy's, carnations and sea lavender. The slight breeze silently whispered through the trees making a relaxing sound. The garden was alive with activity, her son and nephews and nieces playing games, they had all arrived to celebrate her son Anthony's fifth birthday party. Her mum and dad, Norm and his wife Rose along with their twins Alan and Tom, her dad and Norm were playing football with Anthony and the twins, Chrissy glanced over at Rose who was laughing at the antics of her twins. Everyone was surprised when Norm and Rose had started courting, Rose was once Arthur's girlfriend but the relationship had fizzled out after Norm's spell in prison he had not trusted any woman for some time till Rose went to visit May and her mother and their romance had started from there. Over at the table her mum was fussing over May's little girl Anne-Maud who was named after her late gran who had passed away two years ago, Anne-Maud was the image of her mum with her golden locks of hair and large blue eyes, May's husband Gary had to decline the invitation because his father was very ill. Sitting in the other lounger was Gladys, Chrissy had kept in touch with Jimmy's parents after she had Anthony after all they were his grandparents, they were doting grandparents until last year when Albert had collapsed in work from a heart attack, but Gladys still maintained he had died of a broken heart after his son's execution. Tony, Jimmy's mate had left England to start a new life in America with his wife Cissy and young daughter Celia, he hadn't been there a year when he had got involved with the wrong people and had been found violently beaten up and left to die in an alley way, his wife and young daughter had returned home and had since met and married a decent man. After Jimmy's execution, Chrissy went into a world of her own a world of self-torture blaming herself for the events that had happened, she should have given in to his advances after all she knew she loved him, and he loved her. Her brother Norm had come into her bedroom opened the curtains and made her sit up, he had told her to think of all that had happened, she, Chrissy, had not forced him to start a moneymaking scheme, she hadn't forced him to kill three people he had already started on the wrong road to criminal activities long before she had met him again. He had told her she was behaving selfishly not looking after herself or the unborn baby and she was also making their lives miserable by her behaviour. After her brother's straightforward talk Chrissy then concentrated on getting her life back to as normal as possible before her baby was born. When Anthony was born, and she looked into his eyes she made a promise to herself that she would concentrate all her efforts on caring for her son. Chrissy had no interest in other men she still loved Jimmy, she still did if she was honest even though she was now happily married.

Her thoughts were interrupted by her son who ran to her. "Mum. When can we have my birthday cake?"

He was hot and his face was glowing red from running around.

"Have a drink Anthony we will wait till daddy gets home from work."

Her husband had adopted Anthony and gave him his name, Albert had been upset that his grandson would not have the Cartwright name but eventually accepted it would be better if he had the same surname as his parents. Chrissy looked at her son he was the image of his natural father he would be tall as well and now he had started school he was the tallest boy in his class. He loved football and kept boasting to his friends that his uncle Gerry played for Tranmere Rovers even though it was only the reserves. "Ahhh, Mum I wish Uncle Gerry was here to see me score a goal against grandad Bennett."

"Have a drink, Anthony. You need to cool down sit down with grandad and Uncle Norm they look hot as well."

Her dad and Norm sat on the grass and gulped down the iced lemonade, her dad was told off by her mum to behave he wasn't as young as he thought he was everyone laughed. Gladys had risen from her lounger to take the damp tea towels from over the food. "You stay there, Chrissy, love, I'll sort out the sandwiches your hubby will be home soon and will want to eat straight away."

The back-garden gate opened, and a large, uniformed policeman walked in he wore a sergeant's stripe on the sleeve, he also looked hot his skin was tanned and his hair was now a golden blonde bleached by the sun.

"Hi everyone, what a scorcher I'm dying for a cool long drink."

"Daddy, daddy."

Anthony ran to him and wrapped his arms around the large man's legs, he was lifted with one arm and placed on his daddy's shoulder. He laughed, "You look like a beacon with your red face I could use you when the traffic lights stop working."

"I scored a goal against grandad Bennett daddy."

He looked over at his father and brother-in-law who were resting on the grass. "Well done, Anthony, I can see you have knackered your grandad and uncle what about your cousins Alan and Tom?"

He paused then told his daddy they had helped him, Rose told Anthony he was a good boy for letting his cousins take some of the glory.

The policeman walked over to Chrissy who handed him a glass of chilled lemonade which he drank quickly then asked for a refill. "I hope I haven't missed all the food and cake?"

"We have waited for you to come home first Gladys has just taken the towels off the food."

"Then can you light the candles on my cake then blow them out and make a wish, I wish I will grow up and be a football player."

His daddy laughed, "You're not supposed to tell anyone what you wished for, but you will have to eat the food first."

Chrissy struggled out of the lounger then was helped by her husband using his free arm, he put Anthony down then put his arms around his wife's expanded waist he tapped her huge belly. "No sign of the little one making an appearance yet it's over a week now."

Chrissy laughed and looked up into her husband's dark blue eyes, "No sign yet, Arthur."